BOOKS BY EIVEEN WEIMAN

Which Way Courage
It Takes Brains

IT
TAKES
BRAINS

Eiveen Weiman

IT
TAKES
BRAINS

Atheneum New York

[*1982*]

LIBRARY OF CONGRESS CATALOGING IN PUBLICATION DATA

Weiman, Eiveen.   It takes brains.

SUMMARY: Barbara is usually in trouble and doesn't
know why; her parents are too busy with their careers
as surgeons to pay attention to her, but an understanding
teacher changes her life.
[1. Behavior—Fiction. 2. Parent and child—Fiction.
3. School stories.] I. Title.
PZ7.W4355It   [Fic]   81-10805
ISBN 0-689-30896-5   AACR2

Copyright © 1982 by Eiveen Weiman
All rights reserved
Published simultaneously in Canada by
McClelland & Stewart, Ltd.
Composition by American–Stratford Graphic Services, Inc.,
Brattleboro, Vermont
Printed and bound by
Fairfield Graphics, Fairfield, Pennsylvania
Designed by M. M. Ahern
First Edition

*For
Lyle,
Novia,
Kat
and
Tracy*

IT
TAKES
BRAINS

[one]

Barbara Brainard was depressed, and it didn't help that she was aware of the cause. A lot of causes really. Of course, she had a lot to feel good about—Mrs. Mac constantly told her how lucky she was: lucky to have such fine parents, live in such an expensive house, go to such a fancy, private school. But it made no difference. She was lonely. The only time she wasn't was when she had a book to read or when she was pretending. She liked to imagine she was beautiful, like Helen of Troy; or she was saving lives, like Florence Nightingale. They were loved. Why couldn't she be?

It wasn't her fault. She didn't know why. The more she thought about it, the more depressed she became, and the more depressed she became, the more she thought about it. It was a vicious circle; she had read about depression in one of her father's medical journals, but that didn't give her an answer either. Maybe Mrs. Mac loved her, but she was paid to be a companion-housekeeper. If her parents loved her, wouldn't they be home once in a while? Oh, she knew all the stories about doctors' devotion to medicine, still they could find the time if they wanted. Maybe it was because she wasn't pretty; she was skinny, her knees were knobby, and her hair was usually a mess. Her mother, on the other hand, was tall and elegant. She always looked more like an illustration from *Harper's Bazaar* than a thoracic surgeon.

Even school was awful. The kids' murmured chant as she passed rang in her ears.

"Brains! Brains! Can't clean drains!"

The memory made her cover her ears as she huddled alone on the grass beside the tennis court and watched the pairs of players as they flashed decoratively around the macadam. The girls might be terrible players, still they sounded as if they were having a good time. It was a relief when the dismissal bell rang.

Well, it was the end of the week at last. Reaching into the top shelf of her locker, she was thinking that sometimes it was an advantage to be tall, when she overheard Doris and Willie Mae as they walked past; they were concentrating on their conversation, and, perhaps, didn't realize she was there. Or they didn't care.

"I'm having a slumber party next week, Willie Mae. Can you come?"

"Sure thing, I think. I'll have to ask, though."

Their voices faded, and Barbara felt lonelier than ever. Another party, and she wouldn't be asked. She never was. Even if she did think their conversations were limited and shallow, it would still be nice to be asked. Well, she might as well pretend it didn't matter. Squaring her shoulders, she flung back her long braids and marched out the door to the school bus.

As the bus dropped the girls at their various front doors, farewells were exchanged and plans for overnight stays were made. It was all cozy and friendly, except for the lone figure at the back of the bus. Barbara lived in the sprawling stone and redwood house at the end of a cul-de-sac and, consequently, at the end of the bus run. There was no one to wave to her but the bus driver.

His name was Manuel Alfredo Diego Avila Gonzalez; he was married, the father of eight children, and he drove the bus to earn enough money to bring his family up from Mexico. Often Barbara would save part of her lunch to share with him because he had once told her that he didn't eat at all during the day, to save money. She usually came up and sat behind him for the last few blocks to her home. He spoke a broken pidgin English so Barbara had acquired a smattering of Spanish and could understand him quite well. Mrs. Mac didn't approve; she never approved when Barbara struck up an acquaintanceship with tradespeople, but it was a great way to learn things. Manuel told her about life in a small village in Mexico; such poverty, she didn't understand and suspected he might be exaggerating for her benefit. But he showed her about shifting gears on the bus.

Naturally, she couldn't drive it, didn't even dare to sit behind the wheel, although it didn't look too difficult.

Mr. Appina, the fresh-produce man, showed her how to choose ripe avocados and sometimes slipped in an extra banana for her. She learned about freon gas in refrigerators from the repairman, and he showed her how to give her cat vitamin pills. In spite of Mrs. Mac's frowns, it was interesting talking to those people, and Barbara felt she learned a lot.

"Adios, Senorita," said Manuel Alfredo as he smiled broadly, his teeth a startling white below his black moustache.

Barbara waved and slouched up the drive. Having the driver friendly was better than no one; still. . . .

"Barbara?" called a voice from the kitchen.

"It's me, Mrs. Mac," said the girl as she dropped her books and sweater on the entrance table and kicked off her shoes. The house was cool after the warm bus ride and smelled of lemon oil and the citrus trees that lined the front patio. A chocolate odor wafted down the hall. Ah, brownies for a snack, she thought, heading in that direction.

"How was school?" asked Mrs. MacDermott automatically. She looked at Barbara's flushed face. "You look hot. Did you overdo at P.E. again?"

Annoyed, she shook her head. "It was just tennis. You can't play without sweating a little. Besides, the bus was stuffy. I'm okay. What's to eat?" She perched on a stool and tried to look hungry.

6

"First, put away your school stuff," said Mrs. MacDermott firmly. She looked at Barbara's feet. "And your shoes, too. And take your shower."

She sighed and went back down the hall. Mrs. Mac meant what she said.

Her room was the first one in the bedroom wing, which faced west and overlooked the ocean. It was so immaculate, she knew Mrs. Mac had been cleaning again.

Deliberately, Barbara scuffed up the area rug and rumpled the spread as she dropped her books on the desk. Now it was better—lived in. She sat on the window seat, rubbed her bare feet against the fur covering and leaned against the glass while she stared out at the sea.

The warm September sun was still high in the cloudless sky; against the distant horizon, an aircraft carrier, looking like a toy, moved slowly up the coast. There were a few smaller fishing boats scattered here and there on the water. It was a view she was so accustomed to, she didn't really see it anymore; still, it always soothed her to listen to the surf break on the rocks just below and to watch them form in a foamy chain beyond the beach, endlessly building, rolling, breaking. Sometimes she made up stories about the ships that passed and their destinations. Maybe someday she'd be able to sail off on one of them; maybe she'd be the first woman to sail alone around the world.

"Barbara, your snack is ready when you are," called Mrs. Mac from the kitchen.

The housekeeper was already drying the cooking pans when Barbara slid onto the kitchen stool and reached for the brownies.

"Mrs. Mac, don't you ever get tired of cleaning?" said Barbara through a mouthful of brownie.

"Not especially." The housekeeper shrugged. "I don't think about it. Besides, it's what your parents pay me to do."

She was assembling the ingredients for shrimp salad, a favorite of Mrs. Brainard's, when the phone rang. Mrs. Mac answered on the kitchen extension. Cradling the phone on her shoulder, she continued to chop lettuce while she talked. It wasn't a long call. After it was over, she hung up the phone and began to put away the salad.

"Your parents will be late. They'll eat at the hospital, so I'll save the shrimp for lunch tomorrow. Lucky I haven't begun to defrost them yet. You can eat in the kitchen with me."

Barbara nodded and slid off the stool. "So what else is new? They're never home. I hate medicine."

"You shouldn't talk like that. It keeps you in nice clothes and at that fancy school of yours."

"I don't need all the clothes, and I don't need the Academy."

"You didn't do so good at public school, neither," said Mrs. Mac crisply.

Barbara had no answer to this truth. That school had been so boring, she was always being punished for not doing her work. So she went back to her room, with an extra brownie for company. At least there she could curl up on the window seat, feed brownie crumbs to Measle, the cat, and read in peace. There were a few advantages to not having parents around all the time to bug her.

Measle was sunning himself in a warm spot on the window seat, with a bit of shade nearby in case he got too warm. As Barbara picked him up, he began to purr and knead his claws into her shoulder.

"You're glad to see me, aren't you?" she said as she settled on the seat. He stretched along her lap, the pupils in his amber eyes narrowed to thin black slits. His tail moved gently just at the tip to show he was listening.

"Maybe you can't talk, but you at least listen," she said. "You know I hate that dopey school. Of course, I didn't like the public school, either." She began to ponder over that. "I used to like school. Kindergarten and first grade were great. Mrs. Heinz was wonderful." She stroked Measle's fur and blinked back a sharp feeling behind her eyes. "But Mom finished her residency and we moved here." It had been hard, transferring at the end of first grade. The new school wasn't anything like the other; neither were the teachers. Mrs. Neubemeyer was only a few years from retirement. Barbara thought she must have been at least a hundred years old. Anyway, she was mostly interested in having a quiet class. She called on Barbara for answers so often, the kids began to tease and call her teacher's pet. So she stopped volunteering. Then, when ol' Neubemeyer discovered she always finished her classwork early, she doubled the assignments just for Barbara. It wasn't fair. And to make it worse, Mrs. Neubemeyer was also her fourth grade teacher. So Barbara stopped working at all. The memory made her move her leg convulsively so Measle gave her a dirty look and stopped purring. She stroked the top of his head, a favorite spot, and he relaxed again.

That was why her parents transferred her to Weldon's; her grades had been so bad in public school, her mother said, that private school could only be an improvement. But it wasn't. She just didn't fit with the other girls. Already they were preoccupied with fashions, make-up, and boys. They had never accepted her. She tried not to volunteer in class, but they still called her "teacher's pet" or "brains" and the teachers thought she was goofing off.

"What's the use?" she asked Measle fiercely. "When I try, I get into trouble, and when I don't try, I get into trouble. I just don't understand. I wish I was somebody else. Not just anybody—someone who is pretty and—and popular. Maybe I was adopted. Maybe I don't belong in this family at all." She thought about that possibility for a few minutes.

Measle yawned widely, showing small sharp teeth and a rough pink tongue.

"I'm glad I have you," she said, stroking the smooth fur, "but I wish you could talk. Or that I had someone. Mrs. Mac means well, but she only tells me to be nice to everyone all the time. That's impossible. Mother's always at the hospital operating on somebody. You'd think the world was full of people who need cardiac bypasses. And Dad's never home either. I get so sick of being told that there's an emergency. Why can't I be an emergency?" She sniffed.

Supper was early and casual. As usual, when her parents were away, Barbara ate in the kitchen with Mrs. Mac. Afterward, she took a supply of books and went off to her room. Although a color TV sat on the corner of a chest, she preferred to read. Gradually, silence settled over the house like a blanket. Footsteps trudged down the hall; Mrs. Mac's door closed. Faintly, Barbara could hear her TV; soon that, too, ceased.

She closed her book and leaned against the window glass to see the moon. It was a new moon, a small sliver riding low in the dark sky. Below, the surf crashed endlessly and shushed against the rocks. She yawned and kicked off her shoes. No point in waiting for her parents; besides, she was tired. Within half an hour she was asleep.

Saturday morning Barbara spent practicing her crawl in the pool. She wanted to be able to swim a mile without stopping; unfortunately, she always lost count of the laps between fifty-five and sixty-five. It was very frustrating. But the swimming relaxed her.

Vigorously toweling her long hair, she followed Mrs. Mac around the kitchen. "If you put in lobster, would it be lobster louis?" she asked, tasting the dressing with the end of her finger. "Why is it called louis? Was it for Louis of France? I think it needs more onion."

"Don't ask me," said Mrs. MacDermott shrugging. It was her usual answer to Barbara's incessant questions. "There's plenty of onion." She held out some salad plates. "Here. You can set the table. And don't shake your hair around the food or get the table-top damp."

Interpreting this as a request to leave the kitchen, Barbara put the plates on the dining table, set out the silverware, and went back to her room to braid her hair. It combed out heavy, dark and straight, nearly to her waist. Usually she enjoyed having such thick hair; it made her feel special, and she could pretend to be Rapunzel. But when she washed it or went swim-ming, it took forever to dry. Then Mrs. Mac nagged at her about sitting in drafts or catching cold or dripping on the furniture.

As she was fastening clips on the braids, she heard her parents' cars in the drive. Since they often had different schedules, even though they worked at the same hospital, they usually drove separately. Her mother was standing in the entrance hall as Barbara came past. Almost always she envied her mother's looks, from the elegant french coil of her hairdo to the slender feet in high-heeled suede shoes. She looked so —so like a fashion plate; Barbara always felt messy and awkward beside her, rather like her old Raggedy Ann doll that sat on a back shelf.

Instead, she suspected, she was like her father. He was thin and awkward; his hair always stood on end. Even his beard looked like a Brillo pad. When his daughter's behavior puzzled him—which was fre-quently—he peered at her over his glasses like a surprised Scarecrow from Oz. He dressed like a scare-crow, too, a lot of the time. If there was anything to the laws of genetics, why couldn't she have inherited her parents brains—either of them—instead of her father's poor eyesight, awkwardness and mode of dress. She sighed and pulled at her T-shirt.

"Hi, dear. Been swimming?" Jessica Brainard asked vaguely. She kissed the top of Barbara's damp head and laid her car keys on the hall table.

"Hi, Mom. Dad here, too?" Though she longed to have her mother come home, she never knew quite what to say to her. What could you say to a surgeon? Seen any interesting hearts lately?

"Hello, kitten." Griffith Brainard came around from the garage, rumpling his already rumpled hair. He patted her head and threw himself in a chair in the living room. "There's no doubt about it," he said frowning. "That car has a knock. I'd better take it to the garage on Monday."

"Are you sure you didn't leave some stuff in the trunk?" asked his wife. Barbara remembered that, a few months ago, he had forgotten some equipment in the car and then pestered the garageman because he couldn't find anything wrong with the engine.

"No," he said peaceably. "I just checked."

Mrs. MacDermott came in to announce lunch.

It was as usual. Mrs. MacDermott's salad was crisp and tangy; her rolls were fresh and warm; the wine was chilled so there was a faint coating of mist on the glasses. Barbara had iced tea, which she disliked; she would have preferred to have had wine—or at least been offered wine—but no one ever asked her. After a perfunctory "How was school, dear?" her parents' conversation turned completely medical.

The two chatted amicably about their work; of absolutely no interest to Barbara. She ate a little salad, picking out the shrimp, and made tic-tac-toe patterns with her fork while she thought about *The Three Musketeers*, which she was reading. How much of the story was fiction? How much was history? Wouldn't it be lovely to live in the seventeenth century and ride in coaches and have duels fought over her. She found history fascinating. Why, she didn't know. It wasn't remotely related to the study of medicine. Maybe, she thought with a flash of insight, that was why. Her parents rejected her, so she rejected them. Maybe she was really a foundling and didn't belong here at all. She became aware that her mother was speaking to her.

"I had a call from Miss Bizantz yesterday, Barbara." Barbara glanced at her mother, a quick, sliding expression.

"Don't you care what she said?"

She shrugged.

"What's wrong, Jess?" said Griffith raising an eyebrow. "I thought putting her in private school was going to solve all the problems."

"So did I." Jessica moved one shoulder slightly and sipped her wine. "The headmistress practically promised me. But it seems that Barbara's grades have slipped even lower. She doesn't complete her work or she turns in assignments done backwards." She frowned at her daughter. "What's the point? You won't even make it to high school at this rate, let alone college or medical school."

"It was just a joke," said Barbara sulkily. "The test was so easy, I figured she'd catch on."

Jessica's lips thinned as she sighed in exasperation. "Try telling that to Miss Bizantz. Teachers and headmistresses aren't known for a sense of humor. Why can't you just do the work right instead of trying to be a smart aleck?"

"What for? Then they give me that much more."

"Now, Barb," said her father gently. "You must follow the rules. You know that."

She opened her mouth to reply, but before she could say anything, Mrs. Mac came in with the stack of mail. Her parents forgot her as they quickly sorted the envelopes into piles. Barbara lost interest; there was never anything for her except sometimes at Christmas.

"This one's from the clinic in Berea," said Jessica, laying a long business envelope beside Griffith's plate. Her voice was noncommittal. He raised his eyebrows at her faintly as he put down his fork and quickly opened it.

"They suggest next weekend for a conference. Are you available?"

"I'll have to check with Cora on Monday, but I think so." She passed the salad. "Did you see Michelson's X-rays? I'll bet it's—"

Abruptly, Barbara pushed back her chair. "May

I be excused, please?" she said and left the room before either of her parents could reply. Always it was medicine. She was sick of it. Why couldn't she have normal parents who went to bridge parties and talked about things people could understand? It was almost worth running away from home.

She found Measle on the patio and sat down beside him while she thought about running away.

She had run away once, when she was seven. She got as far as the library in the center of La Jolla before Mrs. Mac found her. It accomplished nothing, though. Mrs. Mac reported to Jessica, who laughed and said everyone goes through a rebellious stage at age seven; that it was Barbara's way of expressing independence. Nuts!

She hadn't tried it again because she had realized, there in the library, that she had nowhere else to go and it was getting dark. While she had her allowance in her pocket, she knew it wasn't enough for a hotel, and anyway, a hotel clerk would ask questions. So she was pleased to see Mrs. Mac, who was flustered and worried. She had hoped her mother—or her father—would have been worried, too; it was disappointing to find out Jessica hadn't known about it until that evening.

Now Barbara was eleven and she knew more about running away from TV. If the police had picked her up, she'd probably have been taken to Juvenile Hall—an uncomfortable sounding place from the reports she'd heard. If no one found her, she would have had to spend the night outdoors. Once, over a year ago, she had slipped outside in the middle of the night to see what it was like.

A heavy fog had rolled in from the ocean, making everything wet and clammy. The moon and stars were completely blotted out; in fact, she could see nothing beyond the edge of the patio wall. The sound of the crashing surf beat in her ears, interrupted by the regular, deep call of the fog horn. It was lonesome and somehow frightening to be there, even if it was home. She crept back to bed shivering and gave up thoughts of running away, at least until she was older. Now a year had passed and nothing had changed. She still wasn't old enough.

The trouble was, she was too prudent; she didn't really want to be hungry or thirsty or uncomfortable or have no place to go. Too bad life wasn't more like books. Things always ended neatly there. Heroines were always beautiful and always running away. They didn't get hungry or cold either—well, at least not often. She let her mind slip into the seventeenth century. What could life have been like if she had lived then? If her father had been rich and powerful and they had lived in a castle?

[two]

MONDAY MORNING arrived as it always did. It was going to be hot, too. Why can't we have summer vacation in September when we need it, thought Barbara as she rummaged in her closet for a sleeveless dress. It's stupid to have vacation in June, when it's overcast and chilly, and hold school in September, when the temperature is ninety degrees in the shade. But, at least the classrooms were air-conditioned; that helped a lot. As she shrugged into the dress with its full, print skirt, she thought wistfully about wearing shorts and a T-shirt. It would be much more comfortable, but was against school rules. Not that it would bother her, but Mrs. Mac wouldn't let her out of the house dressed that way.

"Hurry, Barbara. You'll make the bus wait, finish your milk, you look nice," said Mrs. Mac in a single breath as Barbara dawdled over her juice and cereal.

Manuel didn't mind waiting and she hated to rush in the morning. In fact, sometimes, he said, he arrived early so he could enjoy the peace and the sound of the surf. By the time the bus filled with girls, he couldn't hear himself think, even in Spanish. Barbara could see his point.

Doris Eberle and Willie Mae Martin greeted her with smiles when they got on. Doris had a new alpaca sweater that matched her skirt. It was too hot for the sweater, but her father had just brought it back from Peru and Doris wanted to show it off. Barbara admired it and was grateful that they had gotten over their annoyance with her.

"Did you get the math homework done, Brains?" asked Willie Mae.

Barbara nodded and didn't add that she had done it at school while waiting for the others to finish the history test.

"Uh—what did you get for the fourteenth problem? I worked and worked, and I just couldn't get it," said Willie Mae plaintively.

Pulling out the paper, Barbara glanced at it. "Four hours, fifteen minutes," she said. "Did you allow for the acceleration?"

"No." Willie Mae shook her head and glanced at Doris. "I knew you'd have the answer. I just don't understand about acceleration." She sighed. "I wish I was smart like you."

Even to Barbara, her remark rang false. They wished no such thing, but only to copy her work.

Sometime she was going to summon up the nerve to refuse to give anyone the answers. Let them study for a change.

It was a good resolution but hard to keep. When Doris prodded her during the test and whispered, "What's number five?" Barbara moved so that she could see the paper. While she was at it, Doris copied the answers to six and eight as well. Barbara knew it and resented it, but did nothing about it. Mrs. Mac kept telling her she should try harder to have friends. She didn't know any other way to try.

Annoyance with herself and with her classmates who put her in such a position brought on a headache. She went to the rest room for a drink of water and to bathe her face and wrists. Usually that helped. She was behind the closed door of a cubicle out of sight when Doris and four others came into the washroom. She hadn't intended to eavesdrop on Doris or anyone, and when she heard what they said, she was heartily sorry she had.

"Hey, Doris, who else is invited to your slumber party?" asked Willie Mae. She didn't sound so plaintive now.

Doris giggled, a high-pitched giggle that set Barbara's teeth on edge. "Just Marty. That'll make six of us. Mother says no more. The housekeeper is threatening to quit now, if we make any trouble."

"What about Brains?" That was Lana Jefferson. She always drawled. It came from trying to fake a southern accent. Barbara realized she should have shouted or something, to draw attention to herself, but now it was too late. She remained in a frozen huddle behind the door.

"Brains?" Doris's voice rose to a shriek and she giggled again. "What for? She'd just be a wet blanket, pretending she doesn't know the answers so we won't think she's stuck up."

"You're right. We don't want her," said Willie Mae firmly. The voices receded toward the door. "I never did like her."

That was the final straw. Barbara jerked open the cubicle door and strode out. The other girls were by the partly open rest room door. Their faces changed into varying degrees of embarrassment. Doris turned bright pink; Lana put her hand over her mouth. Willie Mae tried to brazen it out.

"Eavesdropping, Brains? Don't you know eavesdroppers only hear bad things about themselves?"

Barbara was almost too angry to talk. Her stomach churned into a hard knot and her throat was tight, but words spilled out anyway.

"I was there first. You're all so stupid you didn't even look around. That's the last time I give you any answers on a math test, Willie Mae. Or you either, Doris. You can all flunk for all I care." She turned to Doris, who was trying to edge through the doorway. "And I wouldn't come to your old slumber party anyway. I've better things to do with my time—like taking out the garbage."

She started to push past Doris, when Willie Mae grabbed her arm.

"Look who's garbage."

Willie Mae gave a hard yank to one of Barbara's braids. Cissy Antonio had been standing silent, but now she stuck out her foot. Barbara tripped. In an effort to keep her balance, she flung herself against Doris. In seconds, they were both rolling on the tile floor, pounding and scratching, their books and papers scattered all over the room.

The fight lasted only a few moments. Someone called the proctor, Miss Nichols, who was also the physical education instructor. She jerked each girl to her feet and marched them to the office of the head-mistress, Miss Bizantz.

"She started it," said Doris, looking innocent. "I was just in the washroom with a couple friends. We were minding our own business when she came in and started to hit me. You can ask Willie Mae or Cissy or Lana."

The unfairness of it made Barbara angrier; she could only shake her head and mutter. She had opened her mouth to protest, however, when the head-mistress began to tap the folder on the desk in front of her. Barbara had no difficulty in recognizing her name, even upside down.

"You're developing quite a stack of cards here, young lady," said Miss Bizantz frowning. She began to shuffle the file cards.

"Writing cartoons on the washroom walls—that was October, last year. You arrived in September. Circulating a petition complaining about the quality of our orchestra—December. Arguing with your teachers —November, December, January. Taking your radio

to school and listening to it instead of Mrs. Farkas—
February. Writing your answers in Spanish, broken
Spanish at that—April. Coming to school in shorts—
May. Yes. You had quite a year, last year. Now here
it is the start of your second year. It doesn't look as if
you've improved much over the summer."

She sighed and wrote on another card. "Barbara,
what are we going to do with you?"

Barbara glared at the floor while the headmistress waited. At last she sighed again. "All right. I
won't notify your parents, at least not this time. Your
punishment will be suspension of your library privileges—that's for both of you—for two weeks. You may
go back to class."

Barbara and Doris walked stiffly from the office,
carefully avoiding each other's gaze. Barbara's knees
hurt where they had hit the tile floor, and the pocket
of her skirt was torn; she had a headache, too. But she
was secretly pleased to see that Doris had a long
scratch down the side of her face and her eye looked
purple and puffy. She was going to have a lovely
shiner.

Doris met the other girls outside and began to
giggle about the punishment. She was relieved because she never went near the library anyway. To
Barbara, it was a genuine deprivation. Two weeks was
a long time. Maybe she could go during lunch today
and take out a couple extra books, to tide her over.

She ate lunch quickly and slipped out of the cafeteria and down the hall to the library. It was a gra-
cious paneled room, with comfortable chairs and good

reading lights for each table. Barbara loved the library and spent as much time there as she could. Miss Wilson, the librarian, sometimes let her shelve books; and she explained the Dewey Decimal system for arranging the nonfiction. Aside from Miss Wilson, the library was empty when Barbara opened the door.

"Why, hello, Barbara. What are you doing here?" said the librarian, raising her eyebrows.

"Hello, Miss Wilson," said Barbara softly. She always unconsciously lowered her voice in the library; maybe it was because Miss Wilson always whispered. "I just thought I'd pick out a couple books —maybe—would it be okay if I took three or four this time? I've got a lot of reading to do."

"I'm sorry," whispered Miss Wilson, shaking her head. "You've had your library privileges suspended for two weeks."

"But—but that's not supposed to be until tomorrow."

"No. I'm sorry. Effective right away. Headmistress sent word."

Silently Barbara turned and walked quietly out of the room and down the hall. She blinked furiously to keep back the tears. It wasn't fair! The one thing about this awful place that she liked and it was taken away. And the fight wasn't even her fault! She couldn't stand it, not for two weeks.

There was still fifteen minutes left of the lunch hour as she came out of the building and stood blinking in the sunshine. Only the older girls, from ninth grade and up, sprawled on the front lawn. It was known as Senior Lawn. Barbara knew she shouldn't be there; she belonged with the younger girls on the other side. But she couldn't, she just couldn't go back to where Doris and Willie Mae were giggling and showing off. She started slowly down the steps to the curving walk that led to the front gate. The other girls were so deep in conversation, no one noticed her.

Then she was outside the gate, outside school grounds. Indecisively, she stood there watching traffic. It wasn't busy in the middle of the day; a few nondescript sedans cruised past, and across the street a couple of fall tourists browsed in store windows.

"I know," she whispered, "I'll go to the library in La Jolla." Even though she had only been there in the evening when Mrs. Mac had taken her, she knew how to find it.

She moved briskly through the afternoon heat. The hurt of the day receded a little as she moved farther from the school. Walking down Pearl Street, Barbara experienced a sense of contentment; the day was sunny and fine and she was doing something she wanted to do. She straightened her shoulders and pretended she was Secret Agent X-9 on the way to an assignment. It was almost as good as being adult. As she passed the Friendly Critter Pet Store, movement in the window caught her eye and she stopped. A litter of six fuzzy white pups rolled and tumbled in the sawdust. According to the sign, they were six-week-old samoyeds for sale for two hundred twenty-five dollars. She sighed and held her palm against the window. One of the pups stood on his hind legs, braced his front paws on the glass and tried to lick her fingers. His tail curled over his back in a tight ringlet and his stomach bulged pinkly, rather like a piglet in an angora sweater. She sighed again and regretfully continued to walk. She wanted a dog so badly. She would have saved her allowance forever, to pay for one. But Mrs. Mac didn't want the mess, and her parents told her she was too young. When she was grown-up, she'd have lots of dogs—all sizes.

She walked on smiling, thinking of the dogs she'd have. It was a mile and a half to the library, so the afternoon was well advanced when Barbara entered the reading room.

It was nowhere near as luxurious as the library at Weldon's, but it had books and that was all that mattered. Looking at her watch, she figured she had an hour before she would need to start back to meet the school bus. Attendance at school was taken in the morning; she probably wouldn't be missed. But it was at least five miles to her home and she had no money for a phone call. So she had better be on that bus at 3:15.

At 2:02, Miss Rose A. Apple, first assistant to Miss Bizantz, walked through the reading room doors, hesitated as she peered through her thick glasses, and then came straight across to Barbara. Barbara pretended not to see her.

Damn, she thought. Another five minutes and she would have been gone. As it was, she finally swallowed and raised her head to stare innocently at Miss Apple, who never looked in the least rosy.

"Why, hello, Miss Apple. Fancy seeing you here."

"All right, Barbara Brainard. You will come along with me. Now!"

"Yes, ma'am." No point in thinking up excuses. She wouldn't have paid attention anyway. Barbara closed the book carefully and stood up. It wouldn't do any good to try to make a joke, either. Miss Apple had no sense of humor, whatsoever. Besides, Barbara didn't really feel like joking. Combined with fighting this morning, leaving school grounds without permission was a very serious offense. Now that she was faced with the consequences, she didn't know why she had done it. She couldn't even say she didn't know the rules—or that it was an emergency. For a brief second, Barbara wished she had Doris's ability to fib—or Lana's. They would have made up some outrageous story that would probably have had old Beeswax apologizing for not trusting them.

Oh well, she thought, as she slid into the back seat of Miss Apple's ten-year-old Plymouth, what's the worst they could do?

Miss Bizantz kept her waiting for half an hour in the outer office and then spoke to her coldly and briefly. Barbara, who had been almost reduced to imagining thumbscrews, was alternately relieved and appalled.

"Your parents will be informed, Barbara. Some action must be taken. We will not tolerate this type of behavior at the academy."

"Yes, ma'am."

27

"For now, you are dismissed; that's your bus loading out front. You will be informed about what's been decided."

"Yes, ma'am," Barbara whispered as she sketched a quick curtsy, something she usually forgot, and left the office.

Her bus was filling up rapidly. Evidently none of the students knew she had left the grounds. They nodded casually as usual and continued their conversations. She sat alone at the back of the bus and thought firmly of nothing at all.

Instead of clomping noisily into the house and demanding a snack when she reached home, Barbara slipped past the front windows and around the garden to the huge podocarpus tree that stood at the north end of the yard. Its graceful branches, with their narrow, lacy leaves, drooped almost to the ground. When her back was against the trunk, she was hidden from the house and could simply sit and think.

As she sank onto the leaves with a rustle, Measle, the cat, uncurled from his spot half in the sun and half in the shade. With an air of indifference, he rubbed against her leg. She lifted him onto her lap and stroked his sleek head. He stretched a bit and began to purr in a tentative way. It was a comforting sound. All she had was Measle. At least she could count on the cat to be her friend. Animals were kinder than people. They didn't pretend to like you and then talk about you behind your back. They were grateful for any attention at all. Her thoughts brought a lump to her throat and tears to her eyes. As one spilled over and ran down her cheek to drip onto the cat's head, he flicked an ear in annoyance.

Life was sure unfair; Barbara clutched her pet tighter. Measle twitched his ears, and the tip of his tail began to flick. She sighed and rustled the leaves with her feet. On the other side of the low wall, the ground dropped steeply away to the rocks below. Waves crashed steadily against them with a continuous, background sound. It was nice under her tree. She was comfortable there. Too bad she had to ever go inside. As she continued to clutch the cat, he squirmed until he worked his way loose, jumped down and stalked across the yard, tail held rigid.

Measle's abandonment was the last straw. Barbara put her head on her knees and began to cry in earnest.

"I wish I was grown-up," she sobbed. "Then I could do as I pleased. It's awful being a kid." She wished she were tall and beautiful like her mother and could wear high heels and French perfume. Not that she'd be a doctor, like her mother. She'd be a famous poet, or writer, or playwright. Then no one would tease her or choose her last for teams or pay no attention to her. She dreaded what her parents would say. Would it be better if they were angry or if they ignored the situation entirely. Either was possible.

Barbara heard her father calling the first time, but she stayed where she was. Why ask for trouble sooner than necessary? Besides, the phone might ring and the confrontation would be postponed. But when he walked to the edge of the patio and could see her under the tree, she accepted the inevitable and stumbled to her feet.

"Did you call, Dad?"

"You know I did." He held the door for her and then followed her into the house. "Your mother and I want to talk to you."

"Oh? What about?"

"Stop playing the innocent. You know what it's about." Her mother spoke sharply, as she often did. Barbara looked down at herself, bloody knees, skirt muddied and hitched around sideways, her hair in a tangle. She was a mess; she looked it and felt it. No wonder her mother always twisted her mouth and frowned at her.

"For goodness sake, put on your glasses. You look blind as a bat that way."

"I can't. I lost them." Barbara fumbled for a pocket as if expecting the glasses to suddenly appear.

"Dammit, Barbara, that's the third pair in three months," said her father explosively. "Where on earth do you leave them?"

"I don't need them," said Barbara sulkily. She really did but somehow the glasses seemed to disappear.

"Never mind that now, Griff." Jessica began tapping her long fingers on the arm of the couch, a sure sign of great annoyance. "I got a call from the headmistress just before I left the office. I'm sure you know why." She swept on, as usual, without waiting for Barbara's answer. "Fighting in school! A great hulk of a girl like you! I could perhaps understand it if you were seven—although it would be bad enough then— but at eleven, it's inexcusable. And as if that's not bad enough, you blithely walk out of the school grounds and wander into La Jolla without asking permission from anyone at all. You know the rules. You know how careful the school is about protecting its students. We rely on that. You can't go off wandering around town. Anything could happen to you."

"I was okay. The fight wasn't my fault, any- way," she mumbled.

"Why, Barb? Just tell us that," said her father. He ran his hand through his hair, rumpling it still more.

"Just—you wouldn't understand." How could she expect someone who was an adult to understand her problem?

"No, we don't understand." Jessica's fingers kept tapping, and she sighed again. "Do you have any idea how humiliating it is to be continually notified that the conduct of my daughter is unacceptable? And that her schoolwork isn't even grade level?" She stared a moment at Barbara, then bit her lip. "I don't know. We've done everything we could. Even put you in private school. It's a good school. We checked on that. But still you misbehave, and you're failing in math and history and barely passing the rest of your sub- jects. Why? You love history—at least you say you do —and you seem intelligent enough at home."

There was a large lump of lead in the bottom of

Barbara's stomach; she hated it when her mother looked so cold and disapproving and her father so bewildered. She stared at the floor and pulled at the sleeve of her dress.

Her father took off his glasses and began to polish them. "Come on, Barb. You've got to have a reason."

"I don't know." It was very hard to keep back the tears, but she wouldn't cry. She wouldn't. Crying was for in private when no one could see her. "School's dumb. They ask the stupidest questions over and over. The kids are dumb. I thought Doris was my friend and she hates me."

"Doris Eberle is the girl she was fighting with," said Jessica. Her husband nodded.

"I hate her. I hate all of them," Barbara muttered darkly.

"Perhaps you don't try to be friends." That was what Mrs. Mac always said, too. Why didn't they look at things from her point of view? Barbara sighed and chewed on a finger.

"Stop that. You'll ruin your hands," said Jessica. She reached over and pulled at Barbara's arm. Barbara jerked away and put her hands behind her back.

Her mother went on talking. "Well, you'll have some time to think things over. Miss Bizantz says you're suspended for the rest of the week. She wanted to make it two weeks, but I soothed her down to one." Barbara continued to stare at the floor as her mother stood up. "Your father and I must be out of town the rest of this week, so you'll be alone with Mrs. Mac-Dermott. You're to give her no trouble. No TV, no friends over. You can spend your time studying. And this time, put down the correct answers, not something you make up. Clear?"

Barbara nodded.

"That's all then."

She escaped to her room. She didn't want dinner. Measle was on the bed, sleeping in a warm, sunny spot on the spread. He only opened one eye sleepily as Barbara threw herself beside him and began to stroke his side.

"That wasn't so bad. Mother and Dad are going to be gone, and I have to stay home. But they're always going somewhere, and I always have to stay home. Mother said no friends and no TV. I don't care. I don't have friends, and I'd rather read anyway.

It didn't turn out to be the punishment that the Brainards and Miss Bizantz had hoped for, although they didn't know that. While her parents were gone, Barbara spent her time reading, *History of the United States Before 1840;* she finished the novels on the English reading list as well and started on the reading list for the seventh grade. The trouble with all those lists was that there was no challenge to them. She preferred the senior girls' reading list, but she wasn't allowed to read those books. They were supposed to be too adult. When she rested between books, she tried to think what it might have been like to live in Colonial America. What if she had entertained General Washington during the war?

All in all it was a very pleasant week. One of the best.

"Wouldn't it be great if I never had to go back?" she asked Measle. The cat stretched on her lap and shut his eyes, purring steadily.

[three]

THE FOLLOWING MONDAY Barbara gritted her teeth, went back to school, survived, and nothing was changed. Her parents returned on schedule. They didn't talk about their trip, at least not within Barbara's hearing. She did notice a change in atmosphere, however. There was nothing exactly definite but sometimes conversation ceased abruptly when she entered a room. And Jessica stopped griping about her senior colleague, a Dr. Joseph Henderson.

Then, about ten days later, Barbara was peacefully reading in her room when her father called. She hadn't even heard him come home, and it was unusual for him to be home so early—at least an hour before dinner. What was even rarer, Jessica sat in the big lounge chair, her feet tucked under her. As Barbara quickly reviewed her behavior for the past week, she noted her parents were holding glasses of champagne. That was a positive note. They wouldn't likely be angry with her—at least not enough to drag her out and scold her—if they were just sitting there drinking. Besides, she hadn't been in trouble for a week. Still a person never knew about adults; they made their own rules. You never knew where you stood.

She slouched into the living room, her shoulders hunched apprehensively, and stared at the vase of flowers on the end table.

Jessica waved her glass gently and motioned toward a chair.

"Here, Barb. Come join us in a toast. We're moving to Ohio. Griff, I think the occasion warrants a bit of champagne for Barbara, too."

He poured a litle champagne into a third goblet and handed it to Barbara. Numbly, she took it, held it up when her mother said, "Here's to tomorrow," and sipped when they did. She didn't like it; it wasn't even sweet. In fact, it was sour. That thought played around with another, that her parents had taken leave of their senses. No they were looking rather pleased with themselves. But it didn't make any sense, not any sense at all.

"I don't understand," she said at last. "Moving? Where? What—what for? How can we?"

"Just like anyone else. People do move, you know." Her father began to polish his glasses and rock back and forth on his heels. "They move all the time. After all, we've only been here about five years. And I've been offered a pretty good situation at a clinic in Berea. That's where your mother and I went last week."

36

"Berea? Where's that?" It sounded like the end of nowhere.

"It's just south of Cleveland, in Ohio," said Jessica. She leaned forward, speaking quickly. "Your father's going to be chief of staff. They have a very good neurosurgery department."

That sounded important all right, but. . . . "What—what about your practice, Mom? You can't move, can you?"

"That's the beauty of this setup. There's an opening in thoracic surgery, too."

Barbara frowned anxiously as she set the goblet down carefully. It wouldn't do to crack one of the best goblets now.

"What about me?"

"What about you? You'll go with us, of course. It shouldn't be any trouble at all to transfer you. And with all the trouble you've been having at school recently, maybe transferring will help. Although, I wish you could show better grades."

"When can we leave?" said Barbara abruptly.

"All of a sudden you're anxious to go?" said Jessica grinning.

"Sure. That school's a drag. I can't use the library except two days a week, even when I don't break a rule. I have to—at least I'm s'posed to—curtsy when old Beeswax enters or leaves a room and say 'yes ma'am' and 'no ma'am' all the time." Her voice dripped with sarcasm. "And Miss Farkas is so afraid someone will flunk in math, she repeats each lesson at least twelve times."

"I'm sure that's an exaggeration, Barb," murmured her father.

"Maybe," she shrugged. "But she goes so slow. And there's a class in personal hygiene that is the absolute pits! We practice giving teas and introducing people. Nuts!"

Jessica shook her head and ran a hand up the back of her head. Fortunately she chose to ignore the flippant reference to the headmistress. "I admit it hasn't been as successful as we had hoped when we put you there." She glanced up at her husband. "But Barb, you weren't doing so well in public school, either."

"No," There was, unfortunately, a great deal of truth in that, she had to admit.

Griffith finished his champagne and set the glass down with a click. "Well, it'll be a new ball of wax for all of us." He moved away with long strides. "And we'll have a busy few weeks. Speaking of which, I have things to do." With a vague smile and nod, he left the room and soon Barbara heard the roar of his car backing out of the drive and fading away up the street.

"We're going to try to get away in a month," said Jessica returning to an earlier question. "I'm not sure we can make it, but we'll try. You'll need to sort the things you won't be taking."

"What won't I be taking?" said Barbara, suddenly tense.

"Oh, things that are worn out or outgrown. In fact, this is a good chance to get rid of stuff that's just taking up room and we'll never use any more. I've wanted to do it for years."

"Oh," said Barbara thoughtfully. She guessed that would be all right—sorting stuff—if she did the choosing for herself.

IT WAS AMAZING how much stuff could accumulate over the years, even in a house with no basement or attic. Mrs. Mac and Jessica began to pack dishes, crystal and medical books, things that were not to be trusted to the movers. Even Griffith sorted books. Barbara decided to devote one Saturday to dividing her toys; she dragged them all into the center of her bedroom and began to divide the boxes and dolls into two piles. At first, it was easy and the giveaway pile grew quickly. She had either outgrown or tired of most of the games. Then she came across her Raggedy Ann doll. Although she hadn't played with it for a long time, it was in good shape; the stuffing was a little limp so that the head flopped sadly and the apron needed washing. She held up the doll and stared at the shoe-button eyes. They stared solemnly back. It seemed disloyal to just discard a doll that had been a close companion. On the other hand, she had definitely outgrown dolls; she never had really played with them. Hesitatingly, she laid it on the discard pile, then on the pile to save, then back on the discard pile. Then she picked it up and went over to her window seat where she curled up to listen to the surf and dream.

39

It was a beautiful day. Barbara had a sense of timelessness as she watched the breakers build, crest in creamy foam and break against the rocks below. As soon as one broke, the next one was building right behind it. It's been doing this since before I was born, she thought, before there was a La Jolla even, and I suppose, it'll be doing it long after I've gone.

Suddenly, it occurred to her that she wouldn't be watching the surf for much longer. Someone else would have her room. And someone else would sit under the podocarpus tree and swim in the pool.

"Who's buying the house?" she asked Mrs. Mac at lunch. "So many people have come through, I've lost track."

"Um. Me, too. But I think it's that professor. The one who's in the medical school at the university."

"Oh." Barbara looked through the window at the moving leaves. "Do they have children? I hope they take care of my tree."

"I'm sure they will," said Mrs. Mac noncommittally. "But you won't care. You'll be seeing new things, doing new things."

"So will you. You've never been to Ohio. I heard you tell Mom."

The housekeeper shook her head. "I told your folks last night. I'm not going."

Shock almost deprived Barbara of speech. She laid down her fork and stared at Mrs. Mac.

"Of course you are. You've got to go."

"No, I don't." She sat down opposite Barbara, reached out and laid a hand on the girl's arm. "I'm sorry. I regret leaving all of you. But, you know, my son and his family live here. I just don't want to be so far away from them. And they don't want me to go either."

"But. . . ." Carefully Barbara laid her fork across her plate and stood up. She tried to swallow past the lump in her throat. "I don't know what I'll —I'll do without. . . ." She realized that Mrs. Mac had tears in her eyes; her glasses glinted oddly in the light.

"I know. It'll be like cutting off a part of my life, too." She managed a tremulous smile. "Tell you what. I'll take care of Measle, if you like."

"Oh, we're not leaving him here." Barbara's voice squeaked in surprise.

"You aren't?" Mrs. Mac raised her eyebrows. "I thought—I gathered that you weren't going to try to take him."

"Yes, we are." First Mrs. Mac, then Measle. Barbara ran outside and flung herself on the ground under the podocarpus tree. Never before had she felt so helpless. Nobody asked her what she wanted. She was just told go here, move there, transfer to this school. Life was unfair. Mrs. Mac had been with the Brainards since before Barbara was born. She was like a mother, almost. Maybe better. Barbara could tell her things she couldn't tell Jessica, who was seldom home. And Measle was the last straw. It was no problem about leaving the academy; she wasn't happy there anyway. She minded, a little, about giving up her room, but even that was possible. It was just a room after all. And evidently she had no choice about Mrs. Mac. But she wasn't going to leave Measle behind, and that was that. He was her sole companion; she depended on him. He depended on her.

As Barbara stared through the foliage, there was a soft meow and the cat walked toward her, picking his way daintily across the strewn leaves. He rubbed his head against her out-stretched arm, accepted having his back stroked and settled down beside her under the tree. His amber eyes regarded her complacently.

"I'm not going to leave you here. I'm not," she said fiercely. She hadn't decided what to do if her parents said no. That would take some thought. She didn't have much to bargain with; it wasn't as if he was a watch cat or anything. He didn't even catch mice; they gave him indigestion.

Her parents came home for an early dinner, which probably meant they would be going back to the hospital. They were deeply involved in turning over their cases to new doctors, and they hardly seemed to taste the food. The housekeeper had gone out to a movie.

"Mrs. Mac said she's not coming with us," said Barbara abruptly.

"What?" said Jessica vaguely. "Oh—yes. She told us last night. I'm sorry. It would be so much easier if she were coming."

"She has a right not to leave her family," said Griffith mildly.

"I know." Jessica sighed. "I don't mean to be unfair. Sure she has a right to stay. But I'll miss her. She's been with us so long, she's part of this family, too."

"I'll miss her, too," said Barbara with a catch in her voice. Then she continued. "She said you wanted to leave Measle, too."

"It's not that we don't want him. But cats don't like to move," said Griffith as he helped himself to an extra serving of salad.

"They don't travel well, either," said Jessica. "Remember when the Morgans moved to Portland? They tried to take the cat, but it ran away the first night."

Clasping her hands tightly in her lap, Barbara leaned forward. She tried to speak calmly, to be adult and firm.

"I can't leave Measle. I just can't. Mrs. Mac isn't going, and he's all I've got. I've had him since he was a k-kitten. I can't go without him." In spite of her efforts, her voice cracked.

"But, Barbara," said her father frowning," you'll just have to. . . ."

"Griff—" Jessica stretched out her hand to touch his arm. "Would it be possible to take the cat?"

"Well . . . I don't see how. You've said so often that airlines don't take care of animals that are shipped. And we plan to fly. Remember."

"I know. . . ." She sipped her coffee and looked thoughtfully at Barbara, who stared back, not daring to open her mouth. "We could drive."

"Drive! That's over two thousand miles. It would take days."

"I know. But we could, couldn't we? It wouldn't be so hard if you and I split the driving."

"I guess so. It would mean changing all our plans."

"I woudn't mind. All it means, really, is cancelling our flight reservations. I haven't been exactly happy about allowing the movers to ship my antique glassware anyway."

"But. . . ."

"I didn't think you wanted to sell the Maserati, either. If we drove the wagon, we could ship the Maserati."

He grimaced and raised one eyebrow at his daughter.

"Okay, Jess. I don't follow your reasoning, but if it's all that important, we'll drive."

Before Barbara could say a word, her mother raised a hand, palm up. "It won't be easy, Barbara. You'll be responsible for Measle—exercising him, feeding him, keeping him in a cage. We can't have him climbing all over the car."

"I'll see to it," promised Barbara fervently. "I will. Maybe Mrs. Mac knows where to get a cage." She would have promised anything to take the cat.

"And I don't want to hear any complaints if he runs away."

"He won't. I know he won't." She spoke more

positively than she felt, but she intended to take very good care of him.

Mrs. Mac did know where to find a cage. Her son had an old one he no longer needed and was glad to pass it along. Barbara cleaned it up and put in fresh carpeting. It looked quite adequate, although Measle examined it with obvious misgivings.

The days passed quickly. With only a token flounce of triumph, Barbara delivered Jessica's letter withdrawing her from the academy and requesting her records. Miss Bizantz and the teachers expressed a surface regret that they probably didn't feel. She didn't much blame them. Now that it was nearly over, she realized that her time at the academy had been mostly a strain on both sides; and she found room in her heart to see their side a little. It wasn't their fault —maybe—that she didn't fit in.

Berea could only be an improvement. She took an enthusiastic interest in helping the movers pack, until it became obvious that they preferred to work alone. At the very last minute she rescued Raggedy Ann from the discard heap and stuffed her into a bottom drawer. They had once been close companions, and she couldn't bear to abandon her.

As they drove away from the only home Barbara could really remember, she knelt on the back seat and stared out the rear window, suddenly reluctant to leave. Already the house looked deserted; the windows were tightly closed and so were the draperies. The yard was unusually empty. All the patio furniture was in the van that had just left. Even their name was missing from the mailbox. It was as if they had never lived there. Barbara felt displaced: not at home in La Jolla, but not at home anywhere else.

It was early in the morning because her father had wanted to get a good start—so the sky was a uniform soft gray; the air was both brisk and soft, an indication of afternoon warmth and brilliance. Faint shadows grayed the brightness of the hibiscus blossoms on the side of the patio. She could barely see the top of the lacy green foliage of the podocarpus tree on the north side. There were no podocarpus trees in Ohio; she knew, because she had asked one of the movers who came from there. If she listened, she could hear the crash of the surf. There wouldn't be any surf in Berea, either.

It would be different, living in Ohio. Some of the girls at the academy had told stories about the snow and ice and rain. It was cold and messy, they said, and they were glad to be away from there. She had seen snow in the distance on the Cuyamaca Mountains in the winter, but no one had ever taken the time to drive her there. What would it be like in Ohio? She blinked very fast, swallowed, and turned around in her seat, wishing that she were grown-up so she could decide where she would live and not be dragged willy-nilly across the continent. In the case beside her, Measle began to shriek.

"Do something about that damned cat," said Griffith. He had to shout to be heard.

"He—he won't keep it up," said Barbara hopefully. "He's not used to traveling, and he probably thinks he's going to the vet."

"Well, he's fast using up the last of his nine lives."

Barbara spoke coaxingly to the cat. He crouched in the back of his cage, the pupils of his eyes narrowed to slits, and glared at the world. Every few seconds he opened his mouth and gave a soul-shattering screech that increased in volume and frequency. Barbara didn't blame her father, her ears hurt, too, but she didn't blame Measle either. She felt like screeching herself. Cautiously, she unlocked the cage and opened the door a crack. Measle eyed the door with the enthusiasm he showed for a tub of water, but after hesitating awhile, he gingerly poked his head out and looked around. Barbara opened the door completely. Measle stepped out, climbed onto her lap, gave himself a thorough bath, stared at the passing landscape impassively for a while, and then curled up and went to sleep. Gently, Barbara stroked his side.

"That's a good Measle," she said to his unconscious head. "You'll like Berea. It'll be fun." She hoped with all her heart that she spoke the truth for both of them.

In the front seat, her parents discussed the various routes and how far they planned to drive in one day. Now that the cat was quiet, they didn't seem to be aware of the back seat at all. They argued amiably about old cases and what the new clinic would be like. Barbara didn't listen; she was engrossed in imagining herself a young woman of the sixteenth century.

47

Life must have been dramatic in those days, full of heroic deeds and danger. Of course, the peasants didn't have it very comfortable, and she guessed that women in general didn't have it so good either. Still, it would be marvelous to ride around the countryside on horseback and wear velvet dresses. Today seemed so—so mundane in comparison.

They spent the first night in Tucson. It was Barbara's first experience with hotels. Measle's too. He headed instantly for the bed and disappeared underneath; coax as hard as she might, he refused to come out. She left his food in a dish on the floor, set out the cat box and went to bed feeling very lonely indeed. She could hear the faint sounds of the TV from her parents' room next door, and sometimes the murmur of their voices. When they said good night, her father had patted her shoulder and said, "You'll be all right, won't you, Barb? We're right next door." To which she had lifted a nonchalant shoulder.

Originally she had viewed the prospect of a week of eating meals—three times a day—in restaurants and staying in a different hotel every night with enthusiasm. And she'd have her own separate room, too. It would be an adventure, as if she were already grown-up. But it wasn't. It was lonesome. Measle was under the bed; her parents had each other and she couldn't bring herself to admit she wanted company. Barbara turned out her light early and lay awake in the darkness worrying. She couldn't even bring herself to pretend.

After a few minutes, she heard faint sounds.

There was a sliding movement and then a *scritch-scritch* in the cat box. Raising her head, she saw the cat's silhouette shadowed against the window. Measle was hungry and exploring. She felt somewhat cheered; especially as, before she fell asleep, the cat jumped on the bed, walked all around it, and settled down at Barbara's feet. He, too, had had an exhausting day. But at least he seemed to have accepted the changing scene.

As they drove eastward the next day, the landscape changed. All the TV documentaries she had seen hadn't prepared Barbara for the actuality. The tropical, almost artificial, lushness of La Jolla gave way to the starkness of the desert beyond the Cuyamaca Mountains. The colors were delicate beiges, lavenders and pinks, and the trees were short and straggly. In the distance floated the purple mountains that never seemed to be any closer no matter how far they drove. Would Ohio look like this? She didn't suppose it would, but she knew it wouldn't look like La Jolla either. A lone coyote ran across the road ahead of the car. It was the only sign of wildlife they had seen all day, except for the buzzard circling in the sky. In its way, Barbara supposed the landscape was beautiful, but she wanted trees and greenery. Suddenly, she was very homesick for the garden back home and the sound of the surf.

In the front seat, her parents paid very little attention to the scenery; they were deep in a discussion of the new clinic, what they knew of it, and making predictions about the future.

As they moved northward through Missouri, Illinois and Indiana, the climate changed perceptibly. After the desert, Missouri seemed vividly green. Trees were taller, as tall as the trees back home, but different. Instead of gray green podocarpus and eucalyptus, there were great tall maples and oaks. Soon the vivid green of the trees changed to flaming red and gold and the air turned chill. Barbara was glad to wear her suede jacket when she was out of the car.

She moved in a sort of vacuum, thinking only of what she was reading. When she finished her book, she started it again; it was easier to let the words pass in front of her eyes than to leave room in her mind for thinking.

Against the vivid blue of the sky floated some puffy white cumulus clouds. A hawk hovered nearly motionless above the road just in front of them. What was it like up there? She had never flown, but she imagined the air would be fresh and cool—maybe cold. How did a bird keep warm? What did the land look like? Did it look like a flat painting? Maybe you could see clear to the Pacific from up there. How could a bird tell how high mountains were? They flew over mountains all the time.

Lines from a poem sprang into her mind. "O, I have shook the surly bonds of earth and sent my craft. . . ."* That's what gravity was, surly bonds. She wished she could shake her bonds and fly—where? That was the trouble. She didn't know.

* "Flight" by W. McGee.

Day followed day, and the station wagon moved steadily eastward; it seemed as if it would never stop, but just keep moving until it slid off the edge of the world. It was almost a letdown, when they stopped at the end of the fifth day outside a hotel, and Jessica, who was driving, sighed and said, "Well, we're here at last."

[four]

WITHIN THREE DAYS Jessica found a house, and in another two had the furniture moved in. It was a very different house from the one they had left, but she declared herself pleased with it; mainly, Barbara felt, because there was a study off the living room that was big enough for the two large oak desks, all the files and even the medical books. Griffith professed not to care where he lived—it was all the same to him. It probably was.

For herself, Barbara wasn't so sure; she didn't think the house felt welcoming. The ceilings were too high, and the halls echoed her footsteps when she walked through them. Oh, it was a handsome house on the outside, a two-story white colonial, with an attic and lovely, graceful pillars to hold up the wide roof over the front porch. Her room overlooked a large yard with what could be a rose garden; now it lay dormant, brown and dead-looking. Maybe it would be better in the spring. Nevertheless, she missed her old room with the view of the Pacific, and she missed Mrs. MacDermott.

Most of all, she dreaded the new school. The awful day arrived the Monday after they moved into the new house. Boxes of dishes were still piled in the dining room. Barbara couldn't find the cartons filled with her school clothes. It would all wait, said her mother, for the new housekeeper. All the medical books, of course, had been found and recataloged, but otherwise things were almost as the movers had left them. They still ate most meals in a restaurant.

"Mother, I can't go to school like this!" Barbara stood in the doorway of the breakfast room wearing the only clean blouse and skirt she could find. It was a brown set she hated.

"Nonsense. Of course you can." Jessica barely glanced up from the journal she was reading.

"I look like a—a child! Look at this hem." It was barely over her knees.

Her mother did look up, sipped her coffee and pursed her lips before replying. "You've got no choice. We don't have a housekeeper yet, and I have to get to the clinic." She tilted her head appraisingly. "You look fine, Barbara. You've grown a bit this year, that's all."

She finished her coffee and stood up. "As a special treat for your first day, I'll drop you at school." She hesitated. "You don't need to have me go in with you, do you?"

"No—no. I suppose not."

"Good. That's a big girl. Come on, I'm late, and I have a full day."

In the car, they were both silent, wrapped in separate thoughts. Barbara looked sideways at her mother's profile. Her hair was coiled in the usual smooth coil; she never wore a hat. But this time, because of the weather, she was wearing fur-lined gloves. Barbara couldn't see whether she was gripping the wheel with tension or not. Probably not. First-day worries wouldn't affect her. She was always so controlled, so certain; Barbara felt a stab of envy as she thought glumly of the day ahead. A new school. Ugh!

It probably wouldn't be any different from back home in California. She still didn't think of Berea, Ohio, as home. Too soon, her mother stopped in front of a building like all other school buildings, except this one had two stories. It didn't need the letters carved in cement across the front, "Thomas Jefferson Elementary School," for them to know it was the place.

"You have your records, Barb?"

"Um." She held up the manila envelope and opened the car door. Jessica patted her shoulder.

"You'll do fine, darling. Knock 'em dead."

"Um. Bye." Barbara slid out of the car and waved as it moved into morning traffic; then she stood alone in a moving sea of children.

Everyone knew each other. They waved, shouted, jostled as they walked, ran, skipped or wandered into the building. Barbara stood rooted to the sidewalk;

she absolutely couldn't move. What if she didn't go? She could ditch school altogether. There were plenty of places to hide, probably, all day. She might even go home. It wasn't too far to walk, and she thought she remembered the way.

Just as she was about to turn away, the bell rang and the crossing guard came across the street shepherding some stragglers ahead of her. She gave Barbara a look that felt all-knowing. She sighed and turned to climb the stone steps. Well, it probably hadn't been such a good idea at that. She wouldn't have gotten away with it. She never did get away with anything. Look at what happened at Weldon's. Besides, she didn't even have a house key yet.

After the bright sunshine, the hall was dark and filled with noise and moving figures. It smelled of varnish, dust and years of use. Like a trapped deer, Barbara huddled against the wall and wished she were anywhere else. Beside her was an open door. Above it was a sign saying "Office." Heart pounding, she moved through the doorway and into the room.

Two secretaries were at the telephones; they paid no attention to the figure standing tentatively in front of the barricade that divided the room. Through an open doorway, Barbara could see into an inner office. The woman who sat there was gray-haired and slender, though not as thin as Miss Bizantz. The name plate on the door said, "Mrs. Diehl, Principal." She didn't glance up at Barbara either.

Finally a stocky girl about Barbara's height, wearing a red and blue plaid skirt, came into the office, leading two small boys. She had short dark hair, a firm chin and walked with a bounce.

"Wait here," she said firmly to the boys. "You can telephone home when there's an empty phone." Leaving the children, she opened the gate importantly and went through to the other side of the barricade. Not knowing what else to do, Barbara waited, first on one foot and then on the other. The girl sorted papers as the secretaries continued to make phone calls. Finally, she seemed to become aware of Barbara.

"Yes? Did you want something?"

"Uh. I guess so. I—ah—I'm new."

"Sure. I knew I didn't know you." She looked Barbara up and down appraisingly; Barbara decided she didn't like her much. Too bossy. "What school you from?"

"Weldon's Academy. Near San Diego."

"California! Gee!"

There was the clattery sound of a receiver being replaced and the office girl—monitor probably—turned.

"Mrs. Masters, Billy Thompson and Jeff Yaminsky forgot their lunch money—again." She frowned at the two boys who appeared unconcerned. "And we have a new student."

Mrs. Masters came over to the barricade and managed to smile at Barbara while she was shaking her head at Billy and Jeff. "Come in, dear. You'll need to see Mrs. Diehl. Do you have your transfer papers?" She shepherded Barbara toward the inner office. "Let

56

the boys phone home, Margery," she threw over her shoulder as she gently pushed Barbara toward the principal.

She found herself seated across the desk from the steadiest gaze she had ever known. Mrs. Diehl probably already knew she had nearly played hooky. She wondered what was written on the records in the sealed envelope she had handed over.

The principal gave no sign; after reading them, flipping through the grade reports and checking the file beside the desk, she looked up and smiled.

"Scared?"

"A-a little." Barbara nodded and swallowed.

"No need to be." Mrs. Diehl leaned back in her chair. "Your parents are both surgeons, I see."

Barbara nodded. "They're at the Midwest General Clinic."

"I see. A fine place. They must be very good." There seemed nothing to say to this. Mrs. Diehl glanced at the papers. "I must say I'm surprised your grades aren't better. Most of our children whose parents are doctors seem to get very good grades. Was your previous school very difficult? It was a private school, I know."

Barbara licked her very dry lips. "Not—not very."

"Well, we have achievement levels here. I think I'll put you in Mrs. Joliet's class. You should get along fine there." She touched the buzzer, and Margery the Monitor, appeared at the door. "Show Barbara to 214, please, Margery. Tell Mrs. Joliet I'll have the records for her by recess."

"Yes, Mrs. Diehl."

Margery led the way down the hall talking constantly. "Mrs. Joliet's nice. Don't let her looks fool you." She looked sideways at Barbara. "Funny. I would have thought you'd be put in Miss McNealy's room."

"Why?"

"Oh, no reason." Margery shrugged. "It's the class I'm in, Room 100." She led the way upstairs. "We don't have many rules here. Don't get to school before eight-thirty. Line up in front of your classroom when the bell rings. Only first and second graders are allowed on the first floor—and Room 100 people. You can buy your lunch or bring it. We have assigned areas for eating and playing after. And—oh yes, there'll be a fire drill this afternoon, but don't tell anyone. It's supposed to be a surprise." She stopped in front of a closed door. "Questions?"

Barbara felt dazed. "Uh—how about books? I don't have any."

"Mrs. Joliet'll get 'em. We have a library, too. Your class is assigned a period a week." She opened the door and half-pushed Barbara ahead of her.

The teacher, who was quite the homeliest woman Barbara had ever seen, stopped talking and gazed at the newcomers.

"She's new, Mrs. Joliet. Barbara—Barbara what?"

"Barbara Brainard."

"And Mrs. Diehl said she'd have the records by recess."

"Thank you, Margery." Mrs. Joliet looked around the room, frowning. "Barbara, you may sit—no, that's Jamie's place. Sit—oh dear, where can we put you?" She stared at Barbara, who stared soberly back. Margery slipped out, closing the door behind her. It had such a final sound. Barbara knew she shouldn't feel trapped, but somehow she did. Finally, the teacher nodded abruptly.

"Sit there in that empty seat, Barbara. We'll have to get another desk for you this afternoon. In the meantime, you can look on with Melanie until we get your books. If you don't understand where we are in math, see me after school."

Barbara sat down, wishing she were invisible, and tried to follow the discussion. The day wore on. At lunchtime, her new classmates crowded round to find out where she came from.

"San Diego, huh! Uh—where's that?" asked a pudgy boy diffidently.

"California, dopey. Anyone knows that." The speaker was an exceedingly thin girl with long black curls, a blue hair ribbon and an arrogant expression.

"Gee! What's it like? Does the sun really always shine?" asked a small blonde. She wore a necklace with the name Serena strung on it.

"Have you ever been to Disneyland?" asked Melanie. When Barbara nodded, she added, "How often?"

"Oh, I don't know. We go—used to go—about twice a year at least." Barbara shrugged elaborately, exaggerating only a little.

"Do—do you know any movie stars?" Serena wanted to know.

The temptation was too great. Seeing their avid faces, Barbara shrugged again nonchalantly.

"Of course. Let's see—there's Dinah Shore and Phyllis Diller and—and Robert Redford. Dinah's really sweet, and Bob is even better-looking in person."

It was gratifying to see the expressions of respect on their faces. She saw no reason to confess that the only place she had ever seen the celebrities was when they visited San Diego for a telecast and Mrs. Mac-Dermott took her to the taping.

"Gosh," someone murmured.

"Huh. How boring." The girl with the blue ribbon stifled a yawn and turned to wander off across the school yard.

"Don't mind Muriel. Her nose is out of joint," said Melanie chuckling.

They continued to ply Barbara with questions about life in California and celebrities she knew. Barbara was happy, and cheerfully answered all questions, making up what she didn't know.

By the time school ended, Barbara was happier than she had been in a long time. The new school was fun after all, she decided. It didn't look as if it would take long to get caught up in classwork, either, a couple of days at the most.

Walking home through the cold, she decided Berea was a very nice town.

The next few days passed smoothly. Her parents were wrapped up in the clinic. They evidently liked it; dinner conversation concerned medical problems, as usual. Barbara didn't listen much; she spent her time thinking up gossipy tidbits about celebrities to entertain her classmates, and beyond asking how school went, her parents left her pretty much alone. She decided she liked Mrs. Joliet, even if she looked so ugly. Margery the Monitor had been right.

Luckily she found several discarded movie magazines in an upstairs closet. They must have been forgotten by the previous owners. The items reported could be passed on as if they were personal experiences of Barbara herself or, sometimes, her parents or friends of hers. In no time, she became the class expert on movie and TV personalities.

Within two weeks Jessica had hired a housekeeper. The woman wasn't at all like Mrs. MacDermott, but she seemed nice. Barbara's mother had reservations because she wasn't much past thirty-five. To Barbara that was old, but her mother worried. However, the housekeeper of a colleague at the clinic had raved over the cleanliness of Mrs. Boehm's house and the delicacy of her pastry. She had suddenly become a widow; she had never earned her living before, and now that she needed an income, housework was all she knew.

So Jessica had decided to take a chance, and Margaretha Boehm became part of the Brainard household. Because she had been born and reared in Hungary, her English was strained, but that didn't matter. She treated dust and dirt as personal enemies. Measle quickly felt at home with her, however. Mrs. Boehm really liked cats, and she often had a bit of liver or kidney put aside for him. If Barbara was late for school and forgot to feed the cat, Mrs. Boehm took care of it. If he was asleep on the couch, she didn't disturb him by vacuuming next to his ears.

At first the housekeeper's passion for cleanliness caused Barbara to complain. She could never find anything. When she put down a sweater or a book, it was immediately put away. Her papers and books were always stacked in the bookrack, including unfinished homework; games were promptly picked up and put in boxes. When Barbara muttered to her mother, Jessica was unsympathetic.

"If you want to know where your things are, keep them picked up."

However, Mrs. Boehm's intention was kind, and she and Barbara soon worked out an amicable arrangement. Mrs. Boehm agreed not to touch Barbara's desk and anything she wanted undisturbed, she left there. Mrs. Boehm was a short, cheerful person with snapping black eyes who loved to chatter in garbled English about her childhood in a comfortable home in Budapest. It took a while, but eventually Barbara was able to understand almost every word. Sometimes Jessica needed her to interpret. It pleased Barbara tremendously to be able to do something her mother couldn't do. And, like Mrs. MacDermott, Mrs. Boehm had a snack and a sympathetic ear when Barbara returned from school in the afternoon.

Suddenly it was Christmas vacation. The weather had been cold, now it turned nasty. If the sun shone in the morning, it snowed in the afternoon; wet snow that plastered the face and windshields and made driving treacherous. Rain turned to sleet, and sleet built up on top of slush in the streets to make walking precarious. Although she knew her classmates were going ice skating, Barbara preferred to curl up with a book. Measle usually lay on a cushion beside her.

"Why you not go out?" Mrs. Boehm wanted to know. She stood, feather duster in hand, hands on plump hips, and regarded Barbara disapprovingly. "Other kids outside on pond."

"I don't want to," said Barbara firmly.

"Is no good—all time stay indoors. Wintertime for outdoors."

"If you must know, I can't skate." She frowned at the housekeeper and settled herself against the cushions.

Mrs. Boehm shook her head vigorously. "Friends teach. You learn."

"Not now." There was no point arguing with her, Barbara found; the housekeeper always had an answer. But she had absolutely no intentions of being forced outside in such rotten weather. Her fingers and toes turned numb within minutes, and they ached when she came back inside. Why go through all that? She shivered and pulled her sweater closer. "I can't go. I—I've got to finish this book."

The housekeeper sniffed disbelievingly and withdrew. In her opinion, no book ever written was worth missing a social event. Barbara settled down to spend the day leisurely with *Around the World in Eighty Days*. Occasionally she looked out the window at the weather. It began to snow again. Altogether a good day to stay inside; maybe her father would build a fire after dinner—always providing he got home for dinner.

She scratched at some window frost with a fingernail. It looked as if there would be snow for Christmas. That might be fun; it would certainly be different. Back in San Diego, she had always gone swimming on Christmas Day. Ah well, different places, different times. Where had she read that? It didn't matter. Berea was feeling more and more like home. School was a lot of fun, after all. She had a couple of new stories to tell the kids when she saw them again.

[five]

CHRISTMAS WAS a happy holiday. There was snow but the sun shone and the world seemed white and sparkling. Jessica received a platinum mink coat from Griffith, and she gave him an alligator fitted instrument case. They gave Mrs. Boehm a bonus check because they didn't know her tastes; she announced she would use it for a new coat she had seen in the May Company window.

Barbara was pleased with a stack of presents that included clothes, a down jacket, a gold locket and charm bracelet and a subscription to a book club. There were no emergency calls and they all had a fine relaxing day together, while Mrs. Boehm visited her sister Olga.

Barbara went back to school after the holiday feeling pleased with herself and life in general. Her celebrity status had diminished somewhat but was still satisfactory. Mrs. Boehm learned of her pretense at knowing movie stars one January Saturday while she ironed and Barbara polished her shoes.

"No good. Not right," she said, thumping the iron with each word.

"Why not?" Barbara flushed with annoyance. "It isn't doing any harm. I don't tell lies—not real ones. Those things happened. At least, the magazines said they did."

The housekeeper shook her head as she folded one of Griffith's favorite shirts, a blue silk. "Not honest. You pretend you something you not. Why? You nice girl—smart. People like you for you. No need tell lies."

"Well—I didn't start it. It just sort of developed and it isn't lying, it's pretending." She rubbed her nose, leaving a black smudge on the tip.

"Someone finds out. Then you got big trouble," said Mrs. Boehm ominously.

"You won't tell, will you?" It suddenly occurred to Barbara that the housekeeper would have friends in town. "Promise you won't tell."

"No. I not tell." She shook her head as she folded the ironing board and put it away. "But lies get found out, and then—ugh!—big trouble." She slammed the closet door to emphasize her point.

The subject was dropped, and Barbara felt sure Mrs. Boehm would never give her away. She was a lady of high principles and always kept her word. But Barbara deeply regretted that she had so obviously disappointed the housekeeper. It became important to regain Mrs. Boehm's high regard. She began to keep her room spotless and went out of her way to run errands. Mrs. Boehm never said anything but Barbara continued to feel guilty just the same.

When she thought about it, she wished she hadn't started making up those stories. It had snowballed to the point that there was no way she could laugh and say she had only been joking. But maybe no one at school would ever know; the situation might die a natural death.

Then late in January, disaster struck. Muriel, of the long curls, went to visit her grandparents for a weekend. The weather was terrible, and because she couldn't be outside, she read whatever was available; her grandmother had a sizable stack of movie magazines. Muriel read a few, made some interesting comparisons in her mind, and returned to school eager to share with her classmates.

Confronted with the evidence, Barbara tried to bluff and deny the obvious; but the rest of the class clearly did not believe her. They were angry at being duped, and in a single day her status fell to zero. As Mrs. Boehm had foretold, there was big trouble.

Firmly excluded by her classmates, the weekdays once more dragged for Barbara. She began to long for the house in La Jolla. And she again began to pretend she was someone else.

"I don't care," she told Measle fiercely one Saturday morning. "I've always been alone. I always will be. I like it that way." The empty feeling in the pit of her stomach gave a lurch, but she ignored it. Purring steadily, the cat regarded her without blinking; he flexed his claws on the bedspread and flicked the end of his tail. Barbara sighed.

"You don't know how lucky you are. Nothing to worry about. You don't even try to catch mice."

"Barbara, come get your ironing," called Mrs. Boehm.

She gave a final pat to Measle and slid off the bed.

"Coming," she shouted. No use getting Mrs. Boehm upset with her, too. Carrying the stack of newly ironed blouses, she stopped to stare out of the front windows. After a short spurt of late January sunshine and thaw, the weather was settling down to a dreary, uncomfortable, cold. Icy rain had covered the partially thawed snow, making walking not only difficult, but dangerous. Traffic was noisier, too; chains clanked and wheels sloshed as they threw the gray-black slop toward curbs and whichever legs couldn't dodge in time. It was a day to sit in front of a fire and read. Unfortunately, she had finished all her library books as well as the latest book club selection.

Still clutching the laundry, she went back to the kitchen.

"Uh—Mrs. Boehm, can you take me to the library?"

"Ah . . ." The housekeeper paused, iron in hand, and thought. "For why? Never mind. I can take. . . . But not now. Busy now."

"Thanks, that's great." Barbara started for the stairs again. "When?"

"After lunch. Much to do before." The house-keeper spoke firmly as she worked.

"Okay." Barbara nodded and left to put away her clothes. It would have been better if she could have gone sooner, but at least she'd get to go. It would give her something to do in the afternoon, and having something to read would take care of the coming week, as well.

But at 12:30, as Barbara was eating a grilled cheese sandwich, the phone rang. At first she could only hear the murmur of Mrs. Boehm's voice, but then there came a startled exclamation in Hungarian. Whatever it was, it didn't seem as if the news was welcome. She was finishing the last of her milk when the housekeeper appeared in the doorway; her face was flushed, and she looked harassed and unhappy as she untied her apron.

"Got to go. Sister Elsa fall. Sprained ankle—maybe break leg. Don't know. Hurt," she said briefly. "Can't go to library."

"Oh," said Barbara blankly. "Isn't—isn't there a neighbor or someone else?" She wasn't feeling very charitable.

"No. I only one." Mrs. Boehm buttoned her coat and tied a kerchief under her chin. "Miz Brainard"—she couldn't seem to call Jessica by her professional title—"be home for supper. I leave note. You big girl. Be okay."

Without waiting for an answer, she scurried out the door and into her car, a fifteen-year-old Ford, and presently was sloshing toward the main street. Standing at a front window, Barbara watched her go; short as Mrs. Boehm was, she had to strain upright to see over the wheel. From a distance, it looked like a child driving.

Mrs. Boehm always made such a job out of driving, thought Barbara; it'll be easier for me 'cause I'm tall. Unhappily, she fiddled with the drapery cord. The afternoon loomed blankly before her. What was there to do? She wandered out to the kitchen. It looked surgically clean; everything was put away. Barbara decided she wasn't hungry anyway; it was too soon after lunch.

There was nothing to do inside. She was tired of solitaire and didn't feel like playing chess alone. Outside the weather was lousy. If she were home in California, she could have spent the afternoon swimming. She felt a stab of longing that brought a lump to her throat and tears to her eyes.

Measle was nowhere to be found, so she couldn't even talk to him. She tried rereading some of her old books, but she had already read them so many times, she had the stories memorized. And pretending was no good. She wasn't a sixteenth century heroine—not even a twentieth century one.

Dissatisfied, she flung *Treasure Island* across the room and turned to look out the windows. Traffic was light, although the rain had stopped, and few cars passed the house. Moisture lay like tears on the glass pane, and it was cold under her cheek.

Her mother's station wagon sat alone on the

drive; Jessica had ridden to work with her husband and hadn't put the car away. Barbara stared at it glumly. If I could only drive, she thought, I could go to the library by myself. She played tic-tac-toe with herself on the damp glass while she stared at the car. Even without trying, she tied herself three times out of three. There was no challenge in that. Actually, there would be more challenge in trying to back the car out of the drive. That was something she had never done.

Of course, she wouldn't she thought; nevertheless, she wondered if her mother had left the car keys in the rack in the kitchen. As she went down the hall, she decided to let fate make the choice. If the keys weren't there, she would reread *Little Women*. If they were, she would—well, she'd see, that's what.

The keys were in the rack. Without stopping to change her mind, she grabbed a jacket, ran down the walk and climbed into the front seat, behind the wheel.

She wasn't quite tall enough to see over the wheel, but by moving the seat as far forward as it would go and bunching her jacket beneath her, she found she could see fairly well, if she sat up straight. The key went in the ignition. That was so simple any idiot could figure it out. Barbara turned it, and the engine throbbed into life.

"Now, I think I've got to shift," she said aloud. At least the station wagon had an automatic clutch. She didn't suppose she could handle her father's Maserati. Then she remembered Manuel Alfredo, the bus driver in California, and his cheerful instructions about how to drive. She moved the gearshift lever to R and stepped gently on the accelerator. The engine roared, but the car didn't move.

"The brake, that's what's next," she said. As she pulled on the emergency lever, the car began to roll slowly backwards.

"I'm moving! I'm really moving!" she whispered grinning. This was something that was a real thrill. She was a secret service agent on an errand of national security.

There was a slight thump as the rear wheels left the drive and rolled into the street. Then the car was in the middle of the road. Startled to see how far she had gone, Barbara released the accelerator pedal, and the engine stalled. Another car came creeping along, hesitated when it came close to the station wagon, then carefully worked its way around and went on down the street; the other driver didn't seem surprised to see someone rather young at the wheel. Maybe she didn't look so young. Or maybe he just paid no attention.

"Maybe he thinks I can drive," she said. "Maybe I can." It was better to talk out loud; it gave her confidence. "But I'd better do something. I can't just stay here in the middle of the street."

The engine started easily; Barbara shifted to D and slowly maneuvered the car until it was heading down the street. It really didn't seem all that difficult, if she went slowly. In fact, she was having the time of her life. She was the Scarlet Pimpernel on her way to rescue some French aristocrats. While she had the car out, she might just as well stop at the library. She could get a couple of books. It wouldn't take long.

While she was the only moving vehicle, driving wasn't hard, but when she turned the corner, there were other cars, and she began to feel pressure. There didn't seem to be enough room for two-way traffic. The cars moved toward her and passed close. At the end of the block, she could see a traffic light. It was green at the moment, but would it stay that way? And what would she do if it didn't? She thought she knew where the brake pedal was, but the other cars seemed to be skidding in the slush. Would she be able to stop. And wasn't there something about signaling? She had no idea what sort of signal to use. Her heart began to pound heavily, and her arms felt heavy; she could hardly steer. Driving wasn't as much fun as she had thought. More than anything, she wanted to get out and run. It felt as if there were a large, heavy stone over her head about to drop.

The traffic light turned red; at the same time, a car behind her honked sharply. Barbara jerked her head and tramped on the accelerator while she automatically turned the wheel to the right, away from the sound . . . into the left front fender of a blue Cadillac parked at the curb.

Metal bent and tore and shrieked in protest, as the two cars came together. Then there was silence as the station wagon stalled. Barbara's head hit the side

73

windows; her knees hit the dashboard. Her only coherent thought was disbelief: I'll wake up at home. This can't be happening to me.

A uniformed patrolman who had been directing traffic up the block opened the door on her side.

Lady, are you hur—why, you're a kid!" he exclaimed sharply. "Come on outa there!" He took hold of Barbara's arm and pulled her roughly from the car. "What's your name, kid?" he asked looming over her like Nemesis.

Dazed from the crack on her head, Barbara allowed herself to be pulled along. Over and above horror, she felt annoyance. What right had that car to be parked there? The driver should have been more careful. It wouldn't have happened otherwise. She heard the patrolman's voice as if from a great distance. Fright and despair hummed in her ears and froze her voice.

It's only a nightmare, she thought; I'll wake up soon. But she didn't wake up; it was real. The patrolman didn't question her further; instead, he thrust her in the patrol car, took the names of the few bystanders, the license numbers of the two cars, and then drove to an antique building with the label City Hall emblazoned in cement across the front.

The car didn't stop in front; instead, it drove around back to a battered-looking heavy, heavy brown door. Inside, it smelled of staleness, cigarette smoke and human misery.

Numbly, Barbara allowed the patrolman to push

her through the door and up to the desk.

"Kid joyriding," he explained tersely to the man behind the desk. "Here's the license numbers. She hit a parked car. Phone for I.D. will ya? She ain't talkin'. I gotta get back on patrol and play with the public some more. Kids! Bah!" He made a disgusted face, looked as if he'd like to spit but thought better of it, and stamped from the room.

As Barbara began to shiver, the officer behind the desk belched and reached for the phone. He spoke briefly and then yawned and pulled out some keys.

"Okay, kid. Come on. We'll put you in here until we get some info. Too bad we don't have a police woman. Let me know if you feel like talkin'." The door shut, and Barbara was alone.

Her head ached so badly she could hardly see, and her legs were trembling. More than anything, she wanted someone who cared. Carefully, she walked over to the pair of straight chairs beside a heavy table and sat down, folding her hands primly in her lap, her feet flat on the floor. She was still sitting there an hour later when the lock clicked, and the door opened. The police sergeant came in carrying a clipboard.

"How ya doin', kid?" he said, looking at the clipboard. "We found out the car you was drivin' belongs to a Jessica Brainard. Haven't been able to get hold of her, though. You ready to give us your name?" He sat down unhurriedly on the other chair, put the clipboard on the table and sat back, folding his arms. He looked tired and patient, as if he could wait forever.

Barbara opened her mouth and tried to talk. Her throat felt tight, and she had to clear her throat and try twice to form words.

"Ah—I—I'm Bar—Barbara Brainard."

"Oh? Any relation to this Jessica Brainard?"

"She's my—my mother."

"I see." He made notes. "Any ID—identification on you?"

She shook her head.

"Um. What were you doin' in the car? You're too young to drive."

"I—I was g—going to the library."

Raising his eyebrows, he made more notes. "You were what? Well, that's a different reason." Then he looked sharply at her. "If you were really headed for the library, where's your library card?"

"I—I forgot it," she said, shaking her head blindly.

Shrugging, he stood up. "Any idea when someone'll be home at yer house? Or where yer parents are? Ya havta stay here until we c'n contact 'em."

Barbara swallowed hard. They'd be so angry; she couldn't decide which parent she'd prefer. Her mother could blaze into anger so quickly and she could be so icily polite; on the other hand, she got over her anger just as quickly; and Barbara knew she would just hate the patient look in her father's eyes and the fact that he would be so disappointed in her. It didn't matter, though. They always told each other everything anyway. So they would both know. But it was unthinkable to call either of them out of surgery. On the other hand, the alternative seemed to be to stay here.

The sergeant waited at the door and watched her.

"They're due home for supper," she said finally. "That might be around six. Are—are you still open then?" The possibility of spending the night in jail just didn't bear thinking about.

"We never close," he said, sounding a little friendlier. "But it would be easier for you if we could get hold of them earlier. Don't you know where they are?"

She nodded faintly. "They—they're at the clinic. But—but they might be operating. They can't be interrupted if they're in surgery."

"They're doctors? Both of 'em?" At Barbara's nod, he said more gently, "Just give me the phone number and we'll see.

He copied it, gave a slight shrug and said, "Make yourself comfortable," as he shut the door. The lock clicked with a final snap that reminded Barbara of the sound of a mousetrap.

Again she was left alone with only her thoughts for company. They weren't welcome thoughts. They weren't very coherent, either. Round and round, like a squirrel in a cage, ran the same refrain: Why? Why did she do such stupid things? Only an idiot would get into the scrapes she did.

While it seemed like a year, it was only an hour before there was the sound of a key in the lock. The sergeant opened the door and stood back to allow someone to enter.

77

Jessica rushed across the room and knelt down in front of her. "Are you all right? What happened? What possessed you to . . . ? And where's Mrs. Boehm?"

"Now, Jess, we'll find that out later. For now, let's see to the formalities." Her father stood in the doorway, looking rumpled, his topcoat thrown over his hospital greens—so he had been in surgery. Barbara swallowed hard as she looked soberly at them. "This isn't the place to go into why Barbara did what she did."

Jessica stood up, brushed her hand across Barbara's forehead and nodded. "You're right, of course. She seems all right." She turned to the sergeant. "Can we get out of here?"

"You do identify her? This is your—ah—daughter?" He carried the clipboard with its collection of papers.

It took only a few minutes for the necessary forms to be signed, and then they were crowded in the Maserati and heading home. And all the while Barbara hadn't spoken, hadn't been able to speak. She crouched in the space behind the front seats and waited for . . . what she didn't know.

"Sorry about the crush," said her father mildly. "We have—had a station wagon, but someone seems to have gone off with it and broken it."

"Don't joke," said Jessica sharply. "This is serious." Her voice cracked; she bit her lip and stared out the window. No one said anything further. Barbara didn't even look out the window, but stared at her knees and reflected that she had never heard her mother sound so upset before.

In the kitchen, Jessica put three TV dinners in the microwave oven and set the table in the breakfast room. It didn't seem to be a time for the dining room. Griffith wandered around, getting in the way. Barbara put out glasses without being told. None of them spoke; it was as if they were automatons. Like a robot, Barbara found she couldn't eat; the food just seemed to stick in her throat. She did manage to drink part of her milk. Her mother didn't seem to be very hungry, either.

Griffith ate as usual, as if he were thinking about something else. Finally, when he finished, he pushed back his plate and looked at the two of them.

"I think maybe now is the time for a discussion." He glanced at their unfinished plates. "At least we've had a chance to have something to eat."

"First, I'd like to know what happened to Mrs. Boehm," said Jessica. "She's supposed to be here."

"I—I think there's a note," said Barbara, speaking with difficulty. "But she went off in such a rush. . . . She got a phone call from someone. Her sister fell and either sprained an ankle or broke her leg. Mrs. Boehm didn't know."

"Well, that's explained," Jessica said. "She expected us to be home by six, so I'm sure she thought you'd be safe until then."

Barbara swallowed and nodded. "She told me."

"Why, Barb?" said Griffith gently. "This isn't just a small prank. You could have been killed. What were you thinking about? Whatever gave you the idea you could drive? You can't, you know."

"I—I was just—" Suddenly it seemed important to try to explain her actions, to try to get her parents to understand. They hadn't been angry; instead they had been truly concerned about her safety. They had come for her as soon as they were called. And, she guessed, they did have a right to an explanation. She swallowed and began again.

"Mrs. Boehm was going to take me to the library. Then she couldn't. And I didn't have anything to do. At first, I was only going to see if I could get the car to move, but then it was in the street, and I couldn't leave it there. So I thought I might as well go to the library while I was out. It wasn't so hard to drive—as long as there weren't any other cars on the street."

Unexpectedly, Jessica grinned. "That was my thought, too, when I first drove. Unfortunately"—she sobered—"that's all part of learning to drive, how to handle traffic. It's one reason why you must be at least sixteen before you can get a learner's permit."

"I'm sorry," Barbara said in a small voice, "that you had to be called out of surgery."

Her mother shook her head. "I wasn't. I was in a meeting for the internal medicine group. But don't you think we would have gone anyway?" She reached out and touched Barbara's arm. She could only bite her lip and shake her head.

"I was just finishing," said Griffith. "It was time I let MacGonigle do some closing anyway."

"Will it cost a whole lot—the damage, I mean?" asked Barbara timidly. Normally, she would expect to have whatever damage she did taken out of her allowance, but probably this was way beyond whatever she could earn.

Griffith shrugged a shoulder. "It won't be cheap, but we won't worry about that. The important thing is that you're not hurt. Kids who pull what you did have gotten killed."

"I know.'" Looking back, she could see what a stupid stunt it had been. The trouble was, she always thought that when it was too late to do anything about it.

"It seems to me we need to have a serious discussion, Barb. We're glad you're not hurt, but you could have been. So could some innocent bystander. That sort of thing mustn't happen again," said Jessica firmly. "Over and above the cost of the damage, we must consider the cause."

Barbara swallowed. Her parents were looking genuinely concerned, and, she had to admit, they did have a right to be angry.

"I don't know why I did it," she said at last. "I know it was stupid—"

"And dangerous."

"And dangerous. I should have stopped to think, but I didn't." She sighed heavily. "Mrs. Boehm had promised to take me to the library. She had to rush to her sister's so she couldn't. I didn't have anything to do, and I was lonely."

"That's really no excuse," said her father. "It would only have been a couple of hours before we got home."

"Maybe. Sometimes—pretty often, in fact—you don't get home until I've gone to bed. Sometimes I don't see either of you for two or three days."

"It's not that bad," said Jessica lifting her hand in protest.

"Yes, it is. How much are you ever home, really?"

Her parents looked at each other soberly. Griffith cleared his throat, took off his glasses and began to polish them.

"Is she right, Jess? We haven't been spending much time here, but I didn't realize. . . ."

"I always thought having a reliable housekeeper would take care of that," said Jessica slowly. "Mrs. McDermott was good to you, Barb. Mrs. Boehm is, too."

"But it's not the same as having your parents around," said Barbara in a small voice. "I was used to it in California. Most of the kids were being raised by housekeepers at Weldon's." She had never put the thought into words before, but deep inside, she had felt that way. "I guess what I'm saying is that I'd like to have you to talk to more of the time."

"I don't think I'm very good at talking to children," said Jessica thoughtfully. "I've never had much experience at it. Mrs. Mac used to do a better job."

"Only because she was the only one around."

"I thought you were having a fine time at this

school," said Griffith. "You said you thought it was—ah—neat."

"That was a while ago." She couldn't quite bring herself to confess the reason for her classmates' rejection.

"So you've been pretty lonely?"

Barbara nodded.

"I can understand that," said her father. "I was lonely in school, too."

"You were? I didn't know that," said Barbara.

"I didn't either," said Jessica.

He nodded as he polished his glasses. "I was lousy at sports. Couldn't see without these. Even in games, where it was safe to wear them, I had terrible eye-hand coordination. Couldn't hit the side of a barn with the bat. It wasn't until I got to college that I really enjoyed school."

"Wow!" said Barbara. Her father began to assume nearly human dimensions. "Me, too."

"How do you mean?" asked Jessica.

"I didn't know what to call it, but it sounds right," said Barbara carefully. "All I know is I always strike out in baseball. Nobody ever wants me on their team. It isn't fair. We never play any of the games I'm good at." She grimaced so that her parents smiled. The tension in the room lessened.

Jessica sighed and recrossed her legs. "I guess even with the best of intentions, people can be at cross purposes. Medicine means a lot to me. I don't intend to give it up. It was too great a struggle to get through and I need the challenge. But I didn't intend to neglect you, Barb. Mrs. MacDermott was doing such a good job—at least I thought so—that you didn't need me. And here we've got Mrs. Boehm." She sighed again.

"Mrs. Mac was great—so is Mrs. Boehm," said Barbara in a small voice. She frowned and pulled at a braid as she tried to straighten out her thoughts. "But it isn't the same. I didn't notice so much in California —maybe I'm older now. Here I mind when you don't come home until after I've gone to bed."

"And we've been pretty involved with the new jobs," said her father ruefully. "I guess we've been away more than we were aware of."

"But maybe good can result from bad," said Jessica briskly. "I can't remember when we've had a chance to talk like this. It's given me some new insight." She hugged Barbara briefly. "I thank you for that, even if we will put you on restriction for your prank today. And, while I can't promise to be home every time you want me, I'll at least try. Will you try, as well, to tell us what's on your mind and not go off and do some wild stunt to gain attention?"

Barbara nodded faintly. "The trouble is, they don't seem wild when I try them." She hesitated. "What restriction are you going to lay on me?"

Jessica made a tent of her fingers as she looked at her husband. "Griff—what do you think?"

He frowned, rubbed the back of his neck and began to pace back and forth around the room.

"The thing is, you see, Barb, this latest prank is too serious to ignore. True, nobody was hurt, but you could have been. Or you could have hurt an innocent bystander." Barbara nodded solemnly and hunched down in her chair. "I think perhaps you ought to have a chance to see what the consequences can be for some people."

Barbara looked puzzled. Jessica wrinkled her forehead.

"You mean the emergency room, Griff? How?"

"She could spend a few hours on the weekend visiting at the clinic. Emergency's always short-handed." Barbara felt appalled. She hadn't expected anything like that. Usually punishment was in the form of no allowance for a while, or not going to the movies. She had always refused any invitation to visit the hospital or clinic where her parents worked; it didn't interest her, and she felt repelled at the idea of being around sick people.

Her father continued to pace and explain. "I was listening to Tom Ridgely the other day. He has three sons, and before he lets any of them have a driver's license, they have to spend a few evenings in the emergency ward. He said it makes them wonderfully cautious drivers."

"But, Dad—"

"Maybe your father has a point," said Jessica thoughtfully. "You're too old to spank, and taking away your allowance or restricting your privileges doesn't seem appropriate. It's time you began to think about the consequences of your actions."

Barbara hoped that her father would forget or change his mind, but he didn't. So the next Friday night and Saturday, she spent in the emergency rooms of the Midwest Clinic, wearing a heavy cotton uniform that crackled when she moved. There was no problem about fitting her into the schedule.

"Sure," said Mrs. Evans when Griffith brought Barbara in. "We can use all the help we can get. You know that, Doctor. We'll put her right to work." And she did.

Barbara filed insurance forms, helped clean up equipment and pushed wheelchairs. All the time part of her was standing in a corner appalled. It wasn't just the bruised and bloody people waiting for help who made her grit her teeth and clench her hands; it was also the stunned faces of the families. Sometimes it was parents, gray-haired and confused; sometimes it was a child who stood clutching someone's sleeve crying. People who had no connection with the accident stood in the hallway and talked in disjointed, numbed voices. Some of them had had to dress so hastily their shoes didn't match; sometimes they wore no socks. She listened to the nurses trying to be sympathetic and efficient at the same time, while people fumbled for insurance policy numbers or telephone numbers; sometimes they broke down and cried.

The party who was most directly concerned often lay bloody and unconscious on the other side of a curtain, unaware of what was happening.

"Just like me," said Barbara to herself. "I haven't been aware of what I've been doing. I'm going to make an effort from now on, to think before I act." She said the same thing to her father on the way home, adding, "I'm never going to drive a car, either."

"Oh, it isn't as bad as that," he said with a quiet chuckle. "We don't want you to be afraid to drive. Just be aware of the responsibilities."

"Oh, I will," she promised fervently. On the way home, she practiced being a resident surgeon on call twenty-four hours a day, but decided being the scientist who discovered a miracle cure, like Dr. Ehrlich, was better.

[six]

BARBARA REALLY TRIED to get along better in school, but it was difficult to remain even-tempered and show model behavior when no one noticed.

The days dragged by, filled with loneliness and boredom.

While it was good that she and her parents were communicating better, they still weren't home much, and anyway, she spent most of her time at school where she was still ostracized. She read some of Emily Dickinson's poetry. The lines, "This is the Hour of Lead—Remembered, if outlived, As Freezing persons recollect the Snow . . ." caught her mind. She wasn't entirely certain of the meaning, but this certainly did seem to be her Hour of Lead, and she felt permanently chilled. Probably she would outlive this time, but it did drag.

Emily Dickinson had lived as a recluse, but that didn't appeal to Barbara. She had discovered the attractiveness of having friends.

The Thursday night after she had been in the emergency room, Griffith came home holding a stiff wire with a bright red ribbon attached. It was a leash for an invisible dog. He'd bought it from a street vendor for her. She loved it, and the next morning she took it to school. Maybe it would attract some notice. When she reached the playground, she carried it in the manner of someone who was using a metal detector and pretended oblivion to her classmates.

"What're ya doin'?" asked Herbie carelessly.

"What does it look like I'm doing? I'm walking my dog," said Barbara nonchalantly.

"Yer what?"

"I'm walking my dog, stupid," repeated Barbara with studied boredom.

"Are not!"

"Am, too. Just because he's invisible, doesn't mean he's not there. I call him Herbie 'cause he's so ugly."

"Yer a liar. Liar, Liar, pants on fire," shouted Herbie angrily.

Others from the class crowded around and began to chant. Suddenly someone pushed and someone hit and soon Barbara was again involved in rolling on the ground kicking and punching. The yard teacher separated them, recognized the combatants and took them to Mrs. Joliet rather than to the office.

The teacher didn't seem surprised to see them dusty, disheveled and red-faced. In fact, she seemed to have been expecting something like this to happen.

Herbie was only too glad to give his side of the

story, that he had been innocently teasing and Barbara had viciously attacked him. Dismissed, he ran outside eagerly to report that 'ole Barbara was in for it this time.

Barbara stood by the teacher's desk feeling actually ill. After all her good resolutions, now this. What was wrong with her?

Finally Mrs. Joliet spoke in a considering sort of voice.

"How much of what Herbie said is the truth, Barbara?"

"Most of it."

"You really said you were. . . . ?"

Barbara nodded slightly. "I said I had an invisible dog, and he called me a liar." She looked around for the wire. Someone had brought it to the classroom and dropped it in the corner. "Here's his leash." She picked up the wire and held it as if there were a dog on the other end.

The teacher stared at the leash and then at Barbara. "I see. Uh—have you had him long?"

Barbara looked at her sharply. There didn't seem to be any laughter in her expression. "Uh—no. I just —uh—got him."

"He looks like a healthy dog to me. Do you have him clipped?"

Barbara relaxed slightly and grinned. "No. He always looks like this."

"Well, I can sympathize with Herbie. You shouldn't have named the dog after him—or punched him in the stomach."

"No—I'm sorry I—I don't know why I said that. And I didn't mean to punch him either."

"I think you should send it home. A dog really doesn't belong at school—even an invisible one. Tell you what"—she began to reach for a folder from the bottom desk drawer—"you go help Miss Peters in the library for an hour or so until I send for you."

"Okay. Thanks, Mrs. Joliet. And I'll send—uh—Herbie home, too." Barbara put the wire on the teacher's desk and went directly to the library. She had no idea what Mrs. Joliet would do. Fighting was as serious in Berea as it had been in San Diego. She was sure of some punishment. What it would be, she didn't know; suspension at the very least probably. That was what made her feel the worst. Now that it looked as if things were going to be better between her and her parents, this had to happen. They'd never have any confidence in her. She decided that she was her own worst enemy. Even pretending didn't help as much as it used to.

Throughout the morning she helped Miss Peters. Working in the library turned out to be fun. Miss Weichel's second grade class came in, and Barbara helped some of the children choose their books. It brought back memories to look at Peter Rabbit, Padington Bear and Curious George: all one time favorites of hers. The morning passed quickly, and Barbara was able to push her worry to the back of her mind. Although, even there, it lay and fermented like a small, rotten apple.

Why did she do such stupid things? She knew the

rules. And why get so mad when stupid Herbie called her a liar? She knew he had no imagination: why couldn't she have laughed it off?

Just before lunch, the phone call summons came, not from Mrs. Joliet but from Mrs. Diehl. Barbara bit her lip, clenched her fists and marched down the hall with her head up. She might be stupid, she reasoned, but nobody was going to call her a coward.

The office secretary merely motioned her through to Mrs. Diehl's office. The principal was at her desk; Mrs. Joliet sat opposite—that might be a good sign. Beside her sat another teacher Barbara didn't recognize.

Mrs. Diehl motioned her to the chair on the other side of the desk.

"Well, Barbara, have you had a chance to think about your behavior?"

"Yes, Mrs. Diehl." She was only able to whisper.

"And what have you decided about it?"

Barbara wet her lips and pulled at her sweater. It bore smudges from the fight with Herbie. What was Mrs. Diehl trying to get her to say? Was she terribly angry? It was impossible to tell her expression behind those glasses.

"I'm sorry I hit him in the stomach," she whispered. That at least was the truth. "I shouldn't have done it."

"Yes. Well, I'm glad you see that." Mrs. Diehl glanced at the other two women. "We've been talking about your problem. Maybe there's a solution." She appeared to consult some file cards. "Mrs. Joliet thinks you might do better in Miss McNealy's room, and Miss McNealy's willing to have you. How does this strike you?"

Barbara looked from one woman to another. Miss McNealy was red haired and no taller than Barbara. Her feet barely touched the floor. She had green eyes that looked enormous behind her heavy glasses. But what was she really like? Mrs. Joliet was kind and sympathetic; all the students adored her. Barbara had completely forgotten that she had once considered Mrs. Joliet ugly. She didn't know anything about Miss McNealy's class. The three women waited. Barbara knew she should say something. She cleared her throat and took a deep breath.

"Uh—I guess it's okay."

Miss McNealy grinned suddenly, and her eyes almost disappeared.

"You're not sure, though. Are you?" Without waiting, she continued, "We do a fair amount of work in Room 100. It's no easy time. You're expected to study. There won't be time for hijinks."

"Uh—I see."

"Still, most of my students seem to get along. Suppose we give it a try, shall we?" She stood up, not much taller than before. "Go clear out your desk. I'll send Margery to help, and she'll bring you to Room 100 and show you where to put your things." With a wave to the others, she walked briskly from the room.

Mrs. Diehl nodded dismissal to Barbara so she went back to her classroom—former classroom—to collect her stuff. The class was at lunch and she was glad to be alone to think. What did it mean? Why was she being sent to another room? Not that she minded changing, under the present circumstances, but it was puzzling. No one mentioned any other punishment, like staying after school or writing a theme on losing one's temper or even suspension. It couldn't be that simple, and yet no other explanation had been given.

And what would the new class be like? Another new class. She sighed thinking of the adjustments ahead. She was getting tired of making adjustments. Would it ever stop?

Miss McNealy couldn't possibly be as nice as Mrs. Joliet. Miss McNealy looked severe with those glasses. And she was short. Barbara had found short teachers often felt they had to be extra severe to command respect. And what was that she said about work? Barbara wouldn't have time for—for hijinks.

That was it! Realization came so swiftly, Barbara had to sit down. That's the punishment, she thought. That's what Miss McNealy's class is—a class in behavior modification, where they put misfits and discipline problems. Oh, ugh! She sighed with dismay. Her parents would be furious; and just when they were trying so hard to be understanding. Misfortune always came in globs.

Just then the door opened, and Margery the Monitor burst in.

"Hi," she burbled. "Mrs. Diehl told me to help you move."

"Hi," said Barbara weakly.

Margery began to stuff pencils into a leftover

lunch sack, talking as she worked. "They should have asked me the first day. I thought you should come to Room 100. Would've saved all this moving around. You won't need those books." She nodded at the stack Barbara had piled up. "Leave them here. We have our own texts." She picked up the notebooks, lowered the lid on the empty desk and grinned. "All set. Bring your boots and coat."

They walked together down the empty corridor.

"Will—will you miss lunch because of me?" asked Barbara.

"Heck no. You won't either. We'll eat later." Barbara had never known anyone so nonchalant about school schedules, even at Weldon's. She also remembered from an earlier remark of the monitor's that Margery, too, was assigned to Room 100. It seemed difficult to believe that they would choose a discipline problem for office monitor, but who could understand how a principal reasoned? Maybe they wanted to keep Margery where they could watch her.

Room 100 was in the old part of the building. It wasn't a large room but it looked different. The first thing she noticed was that there were no desks, only large tables scattered around with straight chairs. There were cabinets along one wall, white curtains at the windows and, in one corner, a small settee on a green carpet with three largish bookshelves filled with books. They didn't look like textbooks, either. There were even several small animals in cages on top of the cabinets. Things began to look up. Barbara decided that she was going to like Room 100.

"Here," said Margery opening one cabinet. "There's room in here for your stuff." The ringing of the tardy bell cut through her words, but she paid no attention. "Come on. We'll eat in the caf. You can meet the rest of the class." She jammed the notebooks and paper bag full of pencils and pens into the cabinet, slammed the door shut and led the way out of the room. Barbara followed meekly. She couldn't think of a thing to say. The cafeteria was at least familiar. The two girls took trays and worked their way along the line. Margery seemed to know everybody; even the cook and cashier knew her by name.

By the time they sat down among Margery's—now Barbara's—classmates, the rest of the students had gone back to class.

The room seemed empty and echoing. Unconsciously, those left lowered their voices.

Margery introduced Barbara casually saying, "You'll learn everyone's names later. We have only fifteen minutes before Miss Chessen is due."

"Miss Chessen?"

" 'Ole Chestnut. She's the French teacher," said the boy on her left. "You sixth-graders have first class. I'm glad I'm only in fourth."

"You should be in sixth, Dwight. You eat too much in your extra time," said the boy opposite grinning. He had a wild shock of red hair and bright blue eyes.

Dwight sighed and patted his undeniably tubby front. "That's because I like food. I'm going to be a gourmet when I grow up."

"You mean gourmand," said someone else.

Lunch progressed easily. Talk flowed around Barbara as she tried to put names to faces. After a few minutes about half the class stood up.

"Come on, Barbara. Time for French," said Margery. She had either been appointed or appointed herself Barbara's guide. She seemed so self-assured that Barbara felt either could be true.

"I can't. I don't know any French," protested Barbara.

"Won't matter. You'll catch on," said the red-haired boy everyone called Ned.

By the time French class was over, Barbara had learned to say *"Bonjour, Mademoiselle. Comment allez-vous?"* with a creditable accent, and the beginning of grammar rules. She had also learned that there were eight sixth-graders, six fifth-graders and four fourth-graders in Room 100. It seemed like a lot of behavior problems, though they didn't act the way behavior problems should act.

There was free half-hour in the afternoon when they could choose what activity they liked. The students at Barbara's table began to question her.

"How do you like us so far?" asked Florence. She was even taller than Barbara and awkward, but her eyes were friendly.

"Uh, fine, I guess."

"What did you do to get put here?" asked Ned. "Or was it an IQ test?"

"She punched Herbie Bratskeller in the stomach."

"Ha! I've wanted to do that all year," said Mary Jane Dvorak, a dainty, little girl with wide blue eyes and short, curly, blonde hair.

"Good thing you didn't. You know what Miss McNealy would say," said Florence.

"Why did you punch Herbie?" asked Mary Jane. "Not that he didn't deserve it on general principles. He teases everyone."

"He called me a liar," said Barbara, mumbling. It seemed now that it was a disgraceful thing to do.

"You shouldn't let that bother you. He calls everyone a liar," said Margery cheerfully.

"Well—uh—I was walking my invisible dog—" said Barbara haltingly.

"Your what?" said several voices.

"My invisible dog. I had a leash out of wire and a red ribbon on the end and—"

"Hey! What a neat idea," said Edward, who had been quiet up to now. "I'll bring my invisible dog on Monday. He's a St. Bernard, and he's invisible 'cause the landlord doesn't allow dogs. What kind's yours?"

"Uh—I hadn't decided," said Barbara startled.

"Mine's a shi-tzu," said Mary Jane immediately.

"You can't even spell it," said Ned.

"Can so," she said and did.

"Let's all bring invisible dogs on Monday. We'll have a dog show at recess," said Margery.

"What will Miss McNealy say?" asked Jeanette.

"She'll think it's funny," said Edward with confidence, "so long as it doesn't interfere with schoolwork."

It was very puzzling to Barbara. She had never met a group of students like this. And where were the discipline problems? She said as much to Margery as they walked together down Elm Street.

"Is that what you thought?" Margery's eyebrows climbed toward her hairline, and she began to laugh. "You poor kid. They should have told you. I thought you knew. We're Majors."

"Majors?" It didn't mean a thing to Barbara.

"We have achievement levels here at Jefferson. Mrs. Joliet's class is sort of low to middle. Miss Mc-Nealy's is at the top." She tried to look nonchalant and failed. "We're supposed to be gifted—though I've my doubts about a couple of us."

"You mean Room 100 is—but I'm not—" gasped Barbara. It didn't make sense. But then, in a funny way, it did. Only she still couldn't comprehend it.

"Someone thinks you are," said Margery succinctly. "I hope you are. It's a fun class. You saw today. We have our own books and classes and even teachers for art and music and French. We get to try some really neat projects. It beats sitting in regular class and being assigned twice as much work because the teachers find out we can finish the assignments in half the time. And it's nice not to have to pretend to be stupid." They walked a short distance in silence. "The only drawback is that the rest of the school snubs us." She bit her lip and pulled her coat up.

"I thought you guys were snubbing us—you always sat away from everyone else," said Barbara.

"Well—maybe we are, a little," Margery acknowledged honestly. "But mostly they make it clear they don't want us around. So we stick together. I think we're closer to each other than some families are. I know I feel that way."

They reached the corner where Margery turned down her street. She gave an abrupt wave and said, "Bye. Don't forget your dog on Monday," and turned quickly away.

Barbara waved back and nodded. She walked the rest of the way almost running. There was so much for her to share with Mrs. Boehm; and she could hardly wait to tell her parents. Boy, wouldn't everybody be surprised. Gifted, hah!

[seven]

Mrs. Boehm showed no surprise at all.

"Knew you smart. Said so," she said, cutting an extra large brownie.

Barbara perched on a kitchen stool chewing; she reached for the second, a glass of chocolate milk in her other hand. There was a thin chocolate moustache on her upper lip. It was sort of disappointing to have the housekeeper so certain of things, even if her confidence was gratifying. Barbara wanted to astonish someone.

"I didn't—neither did Mom or Dad, I bet," she said. "I always got such low grades, they even put me in private school in California. They thought the extra attention would help, but it didn't."

Mrs. Boehm sniffed skeptically. "Jefferson good school. My nephew there," she said proudly. "He get good grades. Going to be dog doctor."

"You mean a veterinarian?" asked Barbara.

"Sure—dog doctor." She put the casserole in the

oven and pointedly looked at the clock. "You set table now. Okay?"

"Okay." Resignedly, Barbara slid off the stool and opened the china cupboard. Sometimes conversation with Mrs. Boehm was heavy-going; she hoped her parents made it home to dinner. They would be surprised at her transfer, she felt. It was like being Alice and growing unexpectedly.

They came in separately, but they came home. Jessica sniffed her hands and shuddered.

"Ugh! I smell like OR."

Griffith held her chair for her and chuckled. "I'm not surprised. You were operating all morning, weren't you? In fact, I'm surprised you're not still watching the monitors."

She stretched her feet under the table and sipped a glass of wine. "I was until just before I left. But her vital signs stabilized a couple of hours ago." She looked at Barbara. "How did school go today?"

Mrs. Boehm brought in the casserole and salad. She thumped the bowls solidly as a signal she had an opinion.

"Yes, Mrs. Boehm?" said Jessica grinning.

"Barbara put in new class today. Why you not know?"

Jessica sighed. "Because I was repairing Marilyn Bourchette's damaged heart. That's why."

Before Barbara could explain, her father interrupted.

"The principal caught me just before lunch. It

seems Barbara got into a little trouble today." He frowned in her direction. "The teacher, Miss—Miss What's-Her-Name—did some checking and thought she might do better in a class called—ah—the Majors."

"Majors! What's that, a discipline class?" said Jessica bitterly. She glared at Barbara as she served the salad. "I thought, after this past weekend, you were going to think before you acted."

"Majors is smart kids. My nephew in Majors," said Mrs. Boehm firmly. She poured the coffee and then stumped back to the kitchen where she preferred to eat and listen to a Hungarian program on the kitchen radio.

Jessica watched her go; she smiled slightly and shook her head. "She sure has opinions." Turning to Barbara, she frowned. "What did she mean?"

"I don't know," said Barbara. "I didn't know her nephew was in Room 100."

"Stop that. You know what I mean. What's this about a room change, and what are Majors?"

"It's the gifted group, Jes," said Griffith smoothly. "Miss What's-Her-Name thinks Barbara's trouble is that she's intelligent. What about that?"

"Well!" Jessica sat back in astonishment. "What do you know? But why didn't they find that out before? They take enough tests, I always thought."

"But some kids don't do well on tests. It's more than that. It's behavior, too, sometimes. And it helps if the school has a gifted cluster; then the teachers are more apt to notice."

"I take it all back, Barb," said Jessica grinning. "It's great. I'm very proud of you."

Barbara began to eat dinner with enthusiasm.

ON MONDAY MORNING, Barbara found a sign hung on a hook at eye level beside the door to Room 100. It read, "Birds Loose. Positively No Admittance." Barbara looked at her watch. Ten minutes to nine. She had a little while before the tardy bell, but what did the sign mean? Where was she supposed to go?

As she hesitated, Dwight came ambling up and greeted her amiably.

"Hi, Barbara. What's new? Why're you out here?"

She pointed to the sign.

"Oh, that." He turned the knob. "It doesn't mean us—except to warn us to be careful. Just get in as fast as you can." He opened the door a crack, peeked in and then slid through, quickly for as chubby a boy as he was. She followed, shutting the door carefully behind her. About half the class was already in the room going about various chores.

A white dove fluttered past Barbara's shoulder to land on Kim Sung, who was standing in the middle of the room, her hand held palm up, a notebook under her arm. The dove selected a seed from the girl's palm and flew off to the coatroom door. Kim glanced at the clock and wrote in the notebook. Dwight paid no attention to the birds; he got out his slide rule, compass and straight ruler and began working with them. A second dove flew across the room and landed on a curtain rod.

Florence was sketching busily; she glanced up at Barbara, still standing just inside the door.

"Hi. Did you bring your dog?"

Silently Barbara held out the wire with the ribbon on it.

"Good. Have him sit on the table here. I'll do him next. I've almost finished with Mary Jane's poodle." She frowned at the pad, used an eraser quickly, frowned again and made some quick passes with charcoal. "Okay." She looked at the drawing, her head tilted sideways. "It'll do. Now what's the dog's breed, please?" She tried to sound very official.

"Uh, I'm not sure." Barbara was not accustomed to having her flights of imagination taken seriously. It made her unsure.

"I know. He's a cross between a dachshund and a retriever." Florence's pencil flew, and shortly she held up a picture. "There. How do you like that?"

Sure enough, the dog in the sketch was black and curly-haired; yet it bore a definite resemblance to a dachshund.

"You're a real artist," said Barbara in amazement.

Florence smiled and shrugged. "It's fun. I enjoy it."

The tardy bell rang but no one paid it any attention. They already seemed to be busy with individual projects. Miss McNealy was at her desk, talking to the red-haired boy, Ned. Pretty soon, he returned to the sixth-grade table and motioned to Barbara.

"Okay. You're next."

Barbara couldn't imagine what there was to talk to the teacher about, but she obediently went to sit beside the big desk. Miss McNealy explained that everyone in the class had a project. Barbara would be expected to work on one that she chose herself but that Miss McNealy approved. She would work on her project whenever she wasn't studying math or French or one of the other regular subjects.

"What are your special interests, Barbara?" she asked.

"Uh, I don't know." She had never given it any thought before.

"Well, what do you like to spend your time doing?" The teacher flipped through some papers. "From your grades, it doesn't look as if math is a special favorite of yours." Barbara shook her head vigorously. Miss McNealy laughed. "Well, it is with some people. Dwight, for instance, and Edward. How about science. Your parents are doctors; do you like to read science books?"

"Not very much." She thought a few moments. "I—I like to read history and fiction, I guess."

"Ah, yes. Well, you might take a look in our library. See if there is a period of history you favor. We also have extra privileges in the school library. When you choose a topic of history—or some other subject—let me know and we'll work out a reading list and a report for you to do. Or maybe you'd like to write some fiction." She shuffled some more among the papers on the desk. "You may take today to make your choice."

Barbara nodded. It sounded fine to her.

"We work on a contract basis here. You sign up on Monday for the work you expect to finish during the week. You can work at your own speed, ask for help whenever you need it. If you goof off—and you probably will, at least for the first few weeks—you stay on Friday afternoon until you finish your work. Understand?" She smiled at Barbara, her eyes bright behind her glasses.

Barbara was elated. This sounded like nothing but play. She signed her contract card for a respectable amount of math, social studies, literature, geography and history. There was no spelling, she was told, unless she made a mistake in written work. There were dictionaries on each table that looked well-used.

Miss McNealy touched the bell on her desk. There was a faint chime and instantly all the buzz in the room stopped.

"We'll have our circle now, people," she said.

There was a confusion of movement as work was abandoned and a circle of chairs was formed. Kim put the doves in their cages and brought her notebook with her to the circle. Barbara watched with amazement. Somehow, short as she was, Miss McNealy controlled the class. No one dallied; everyone went about his own business. Yet within a minute or two, everyone was seated and waiting.

The discussion that followed covered a multitude of topics. Barbara couldn't tell when they shifted from social studies to science to literature. Kim reported her success—relatively slight—with teaching the doves to identify her as a food source. It was a clear, straightforward report. Florence showed her sketches of the invisible dogs and gave a report on the uses of different working dogs along with their differing personalities. Everyone wanted to have an invisible dog show at lunch and Miss McNealy gave permission. Then followed a discussion of imagination —the difference between that and lying, and the need to know the difference. Barbara found that she had a lot to think about when the group broke up for math lessons.

As soon as she could, she curled up on the settee in the corner library with a history book. It was about the Civil War; she decided she would study that part of history for her project. It was colorful and she could read *Gone With the Wind* as part of the report, maybe. She spent the afternoon happily reading. She wished she was beautiful like Scarlett. What would it have been like to be Scarlett?

On the way home, she asked Margery why the class always responded so quickly when Miss McNealy touched her bell. She never had to touch it twice, and she never raised her voice.

"I dunno," said Ned, who was walking with them. "I'm bigger than she is, but there's a power behind her that's bigger than I am."

Margery rubbed her hands to warm them before tucking them into her jacket pockets. "Don't mind him. He's being ridiculous. But in a way, he's right."

They walked nearly half a block before she continued to talk. "Somehow without trying—or appearing to try—she makes you want to please her. She works really hard helping us. We just try to return the favor."

"Not only that," said Ned, "the stuff is interesting. I don't mind studying when it means something and isn't just a stupid repetition of what I did yesterday. I have a sense of accomplishment."

"That's it; I guess we all do," said Margery firmly.

When approached, Mrs. Boehm merely shrugged and said, "She good teacher." Barbara couldn't really figure it out, but she found herself responding as quickly as the others to the bell. A few times she attempted small practical jokes. Once she let one of the doves out unexpectedly. Kim didn't say a word; she simply held out her hand with some seed in it, and when the dove lighted, she carried it to the cage. She didn't even glance at Barbara, who felt very put down. It was no fun to do tricks when no one reacted.

Reading whenever she wanted was a great deal of fun, too. But then it was Friday. Miss McNealy compared her signed contract to the written work she had turned in and grimaced slightly.

"Well, Barbara, if you want to get home for supper, you'd better get busy. Margery will phone your home and tell them you'll be late."

"But, Miss McNealy. . . ."

"I'm sorry, Barbara. Truly I am. But you did sign a contract."

She sighed and picked up her pen. Later she walked home alone in the gathering darkness. She had learned something else that day: she was expected to keep her word and plan her time. As Miss McNealy pointed out, if she did nothing but read history all week, then she would be spending all Friday afternoon doing math and the other things. Of course, she could always sign up for less on Monday morning, but her pride wouldn't let her. If the others could do the work, then she could too. But, as Hercule Poirot said, it gave her furiously to think.

Winter dragged along with cold, dry weather. Barbara was tired of heavy clothing, and every time there was a wind from the south, she sniffed the air and asked Mrs. Boehm whether she thought spring would be early.

The housekeeper always shook her head and said, "Still time for one more storm. You see. We not have enough snow yet."

It started as rain on a Friday afternoon and turned to sleet as the temperature dropped. Griffith came home, shook his coat, rubbed his hands and announced it was a good night for a fire, maybe even popcorn.

"I'll make hot chocolate," said Jessica enthusiastically.

Mrs. Boehm was visiting her sister Elsa and wouldn't return until morning, so Jessica put on a woolen housecoat and began to rummage in the kitchen. Barbara located the bitter chocolate and some marshmallows Mrs. Boehm kept hidden, and soon the three Brainards were sitting before a crackling fire sipping hot chocolate. Measle curled himself on Barbara's lap purring and nibbling an occasional piece of popcorn. It was just like *Little Women*.

"Great night to be indoors," said Griffith comfortably. "Hope I don't get called out."

"Me, too," said Jessica holding her hands to the fire.

The sleet beat rhythmically against the windows, and the wind shrieked down the drainpipe. It had stopped by the time Barbara went to bed. She lay under the electric blanket and listened to the quiet, thinking how nice an evening could be even when the weather was rotten. She hoped the storm would be over by morning, though; there was shopping she wanted to do, if Mrs. Boehm would take her to the store.

By morning, the storm had passed, but it had left a snowfall of eight inches on the ground. There was also frost on the windows: a lovely, delicate tracing of cold lace. As Barbara scratched at it with a fingernail, the downstairs door banged open and shut and she saw the cat picking his way across the yard, leaving a trail of telltale cat prints in the snow. After each step, he shook a paw vigorously. He reached the shelter of the garage overhang, turned the corner and disappeared.

He won't be out long, she thought. He hates snow. So do I. Not only that, but there goes shopping. But—oh, isn't it beautiful! She gasped as the sun suddenly came out, turning the yard into fairyland. Each shrub wore a smooth ermine overcoat, while tree branches and garage roof sparkled with cascades of diamond icicles. The scene was so brilliant, she had to squint.

Mrs. Boehm was in the kitchen doing her Saturday baking. She told Barbara her parents had gone to the clinic as usual.

"For why, I not know," she muttered darkly. "Bad weather. Should stay home." Her rolling pin thumped vigorously on the inoffensive dough.

"People are sick in bad weather, too," said Barbara philosophically. "Though sometimes I wish. . . ."

The ringing of the doorbell interrupted her. Mrs. Boehm lifted floury hands in a wordless gesture. Barbara slid from the stool. She shivered going down the hall; it was cold except in the kitchen. Darn winter anyway. A boy's stocking cap showed through the frost on the front window. It was probably the paper boy. She scooped up a handful of change from the desk before she opened the door to see Ned Ferris.

"Ned. I thought it was the paper boy," she said opening the door wider. It seemed necessary to apologize for the money in her hand.

"Oh hi, Barbara. It is." He stamped his feet on the mat, stepped inside and carefully shut the door. "I deliver the morning *Plain Dealer*." He pulled off his gloves and rubbed his hands briskly. "It's good to get inside for a little while."

She suddenly felt very shy and held out the money. "I don't know how much it is."

He took some coins, gave her a few pennies in

change, tucked the money in an inside pocket and began to fill out a receipt. "How come you aren't sliding on North Hill?"

"Sliding? Where?"

"North Hill. It's just over there." He jerked his head in the direction he meant. "It's an entrance to Metropolitan Park, and it's closed to traffic when there's snow. It's real good saucering. Our whole group's probably there. I would be, too, but I've got to collect."

"Oh." Barbara shifted her feet and pulled at her sweater. "I can't—that is, I've never. . . ."

"Can't what? Slide on a saucer?" He shook his head. "You've just never tried. Get your coat and stuff. I'm going that way anyway. I'll show you where it is."

"I'd be lousy. My feet get numb right away." Actually she did want to go, but was afraid to say so.

He seemed to sense it. "Just keep moving. It's easy. My kid sisters can do it. They're probably there, too. Come on. Don't be chicken." He turned to the door.

"Well—okay. But . . . just a minute." She ran upstairs for her down jacket.

"Will I need an extra sweater?" She leaned over the bannister to ask.

He shook his head. "Naw. It's not that cold. Too much clothing hampers movement."

Together they walked down the drive, and a few minutes later, they were crunching down the street toward North Hill. Early morning traffic had not yet laid its blanket of black soot on the snow, so the streets were still clean and white. A few cars drove slowly past, chains clinking and wheels creaking. Barbara exhaled, and her breath was a steamy cloud like the exhaust fumes.

"Well, it may not be cold to you, but I'd sure hate to be without a coat," she said.

He chuckled. "I'd know you were from a warm climate. Just wait until you've slid down hill and walked up a few times. You'll be panting."

"Hey—I don't have anything to slide on." What was the point in going if she had to stand around and get chilled?

"No problem. Someone always has an extra one," said Ned shrugging.

They came to a sign, "Cleveland Metropolitan Park—North Hill Entrance."

"Here we are." Ned waved to a plain figure leaning against the sign. "There's Florence."

Florence didn't wave back, but as they came closer, Barbara could see her face was flushed and she was breathing hard.

"Hi," she panted, still leaning against the sign.

"How is it? Good sliding?" asked Ned.

"Fine. Nicely packed. Hi, Barbara. You sliding?" She spoke in short gasps.

"Ah—"

"Yes, she is—if there's an extra saucer," said Ned firmly. "I can't yet. Have to finish collecting." He gave a half wave, nodded and went on down the street. Florence pulled herself away from the post.

114

"I was just on my way home. Have to baby-sit my nieces. But I'll show you where the gang is."

Now that they were nearly there, she felt a wave of trepidation. "Is it hard? I've never gone sliding."

"Heck no. Just watch someone once. You can borrow my saucer. Dwight's using it now, I think."

They came to the curve where the road dropped away in a long, sloping, snow-covered hill. The park was heavily wooded, so great tall pines and oaks blocked out much of the brightness. In the shadows, figures clustered; two or three, sitting on large aluminum saucer-shaped disks, whirled merrily away toward a bottom that was almost out of sight.

"Hi, Dwight," shouted Florence. "Barbara's here. She's gonna use my saucer, too."

A squarish figure in a bright red down jacket turned toward them.

"Well—if Dwight's using it—"

"Hi," said Dwight; he was panting, too. "Sure. I wanta rest anyway." He handed the saucer to Barbara and sat down on a nearby log. "Take your time. I need to catch my breath."

"See how Paul's doing it." Florence pointed. "Just sit down. Take hold of the handles and push yourself off. There's no traffic, but stay away from the shrubbery. You can get scratched up pretty bad there."

Barbara did as she was told; Florence gave her a push to start, and she was off. She moved slowly at first and stayed in the channel worn by earlier saucers. Paul and Douglas passed her, trudging toward the top. They waved and called cheerfully as she slid past, moving faster. The saucer began to turn and pick up speed. Cold air fanned her cheeks; snowflakes brushed her face. She lost all sense of direction as she and the saucer whirled, still headed down hill.

Then voices shouted, "Bail out! Bail out!"

She did the only thing she could think of. She let loose of the handles and flung herself sideways into a snowbank. Mary Jane and the Smith twins pulled her out, laughing.

"Hey! You did great! Isn't this fun?"

It really was, Barbara realized with surprise. The snow was icy down the back of her neck and her leg hurt where it must have banged into something when she went off the saucer. She could hardly get her breath either. But the cold air was stimulating; the sense of speed exhilarating. Even falling into a snowbank didn't really hurt. After three or four hikes up the hill, she found, like the others, she, too, was panting and had half unzipped her jacket.

"Gee, I never knew what I was missing," she said to Ardyth and Douglas as she leaned against a tree panting.

After a while, when she could hardly put one foot in front of the other, Edward announced that it was nearly time for lunch.

"Can you come back after lunch?" asked Ardyth panting. "I am."

Barbara nodded. "Sure thing."

"It'll be more crowded," said Dwight. "We're

the only ones who get up in the morning. Others come in the afternoon."

"Still, it's fun." Douglas zipped his jacket with a snap.

So Barbara returned to the hill after lunch and was greeted with enthusiasm. As Dwight had predicted, other boys and girls appeared lugging saucers and sleds. Soon the snowy slope was speckled with rapidly moving figures.

It was the shortest afternoon Barbara could remember. Before she was nearly ready, the sun sank behind the trees. Reluctantly, everyone gathered up discarded scarves and sweaters. Dwight took the saucer they had shared because he lived near Florence, and the group separated. Barbara walked home alone in the near darkness, yet feeling more accepted than she ever had before.

[eight]

THE NEXT FEW WEEKS were exceedingly busy. Barbara found that Miss McNealy was right: she had no time for pranks. She also found she had lost the inclination. There was more fun to be had in class discussions and arguments, and she had to study to keep up her end. She took part in one debate on how the South lost the Civil War and another one on whether Grant was a great general or a lucky one. Good preparation meant a lot of reading and note-taking and when her side won, she felt a great surge of triumph. The group celebrated with milkshakes at The Hut after school. Florence led the losing side and they joined in just for fun.

It was a shock to Barbara to discover she was behind in math. In other grades she had always been ahead even though she didn't do especially well; but Miss McNealy's sixth grade had finished the state text and was partway through a geometry book.

Since she had never studied geometry, Edward was assigned to tutor her. While it would never be her favorite subject, it was a lot better than the interminable rows of long division and decimals that she had been doing before. But though Edward was patient and his explanations were easily understandable, she still had to do a lot of homework to catch up. For the first time in her life, she was required to study and to think. It was at the same time both frightening and stimulating. But it was also immensely satisfying to be able to meet the challenge.

The week before spring vacation Margery gave a slumber party. She invited Barbara as they headed home after school.

"Sure, I'll come. That is, I'm pretty sure I can." It was raining hard, and the girls hunched over to protect their books. "Who all's coming?"

Margery looked surprised. "All the girls, of course." She giggled. "I tried to ask the boys, but Mom wouldn't let me."

Barbara laughed, too. "That's a shame."

"Oh well, there wouldn't be room. There'll be nine of us as it is." She sighed with pretended regret.

"The fourth and fifth-grade girls are coming?"

Margery nodded. "We always ask everyone. When I was in fourth-grade, we once had a class discussion on being left out. Miss McNealy pointed out that everyone feels that way sometimes, and if, when there are parties or team choosing, we choose only favorites, a lot of nice people can have hurt feelings.

That was her first year here so maybe she was feeling left out. Anyway, we've been acting as a group ever since. Dwight had a Halloween party last fall, and all fifteen of us went to that. By the way, you have a sleeping bag, don't you? We don't have enough beds."

"Sure." Barbara gave a passing thought to Doris Eberle's slumber party, the one to which she hadn't been invited. It seemed very long ago, a time not to be regretted—in spite of today's weather.

Margery carefully avoided a puddle. "Not only that, but look at all the trouble it saves with invitations." They had come to the corner where they separated, and with a wave, Margery turned down her street. Barbara watched her splashing along, head down, clutching her books and grinned. She wasn't bossy at all. In fact, Margery had become a very good friend; but then the whole class had. It was with real surprise that she realized that she genuinely liked everyone in the class; even the Kane sisters, who were so fat, and Mary Jane who spent all her time combing her curls. They were friendly, a lot of fun, and most of the time, kind to each other. They had been very welcoming to her, and she decided she wanted to do something to show her appreciation.

"I want to give a party," she told Mrs. Boehm when she got home.

The housekeeper eyed her suspiciously. "What kind of party?"

Barbara teetered back and forth on the kitchen stool. "Oh, I don't know. How about a—an end of school party?"

"Daytime?" Mrs. Boehm grabbed the stool to keep it upright.

"Um. Maybe. Maybe it could be an evening party. There'd be fifteen of us."

The housekeeper lifted a pot cover, sniffed at the steam and stirred the contents carefully; then she shook the spoon at Barbara.

"I no care. Daytime. Nighttime, fifteen—twenty. No matter. But you gotta ask Mis—ah—Dr. Brainard —that is, you mama."

"Sure. I'll ask tonight. Mom won't care," said Barbara cheerfully. "She probably won't even be here."

Jessica not only didn't mind, she was delighted with Barbara's growing social life. She gave permission for her to attend Margery's slumber party as well as for the end of school party.

"So long as it's all right with Mrs. Boehm," she said.

The housekeeper served dinner briskly. "Okay doke by me," she said cheerfully. "Like kids. Like hustle-bustle."

"I hope you still think so after the party," said Jessica with a wry smile.

Barbara was busy with plans. She could hardly wait to tell Margery and ask her advice.

The next day Margery said she thought it was a marvelous idea.

"We always have a picnic—go to the amusement park or something, on the last day. We could do that and then finish at your house."

That sounded fine to Barbara; they decided to work out further plans during Margery's slumber party.

Although she hadn't been to very many, this one seemed to Barbara to be a big success. The girls curled each other's hair and manicured nails. Mary Jane showed everyone how to do a French braid and announced that Barbara was the only one with hair long enough to make it look really effective. They talked and giggled until two a.m., when Emmy Lou and the Kane twins couldn't help themselves and fell asleep. Florence then suggested that the rest of them ought to follow the example of the younger girls. Tomorrow would be busy because they were going to the zoo and a movie. Soon the family room was quiet, each girl zipped into a sleeping bag and wrapped in individual dreams.

Barbara lay awake for a while, thinking drowsily of an earlier conversation. Somehow the talk had turned to nicknames. She had revealed that her nickname had been Brains and that she hated it.

"Why?" asked Kim. "With Brainard as your last name, I should think it would be obvious."

"It was the way they said it, I guess," said Barbara. She couldn't really remember any more why it had upset her so.

Florence nodded. "I can understand that. If it's a friend, I don't mind being called Ski, but no one else had better do it."

Barbara guessed that the Brains nickname would take hold again; but somehow, this time she didn't mind.

She raised her head to peer through the dim light from the street lamps; even in the dark, she could make out the lumpy forms in sleeping bags. It was a small room. The furniture was shabby. The couch definitely needed reupholstering, and the drapes had looked faded. But nobody really noticed, Margery least of all. They had all had a lot of fun, laughing and teasing and telling jokes. It was one of the best times Barbara could remember. That Florence could sure tell funny stories, some of them at her own expense. Barbara smiled, turned over and slept without dreaming.

SUDDENLY, the week after the slumber party, spring arrived and with it the first days of warmer weather. Overnight, crocus popped into bloom and forsythia bushes changed from straggly brown branches to delicate cascades of yellow. The lawn began to grow as if it intended to become six feet high. Barbara came down to breakfast one morning and found her mother staring through the window at the shaggy grass.

"There's no way to avoid it," she said. "We need a gardener." She sat down and buttered a fresh cinnamon roll.

"Uh," said Griffith, his attention on a medical journal as he stirred his coffee.

"Will you hire one or shall I?" she asked raising her voice.

"Sure, dear. Anytime."

"Griff, you're not listening." This time she poked his foot with her slipper.

"Yes I am." He looked up vaguely. "Something

about the garden." He looked out the window and smiled. "It certainly is beautiful here in the spring, once the snow melts."

"But the grass needs cutting."

"Of course it does. I remember how fast it grew in the spring when I was a kid. Wow! Every week. . . ." He sipped the coffee, his expression nostalgic.

She sighed. "That's what I'm saying. I can't do it. You can't do it. We need a gardener."

He returned to the present. "I suppose we do. Have you someone in mind?"

"No." She finished her roll and slid back her chair. "I thought I'd call an agency. The trouble is I won't have time to do any interviewing. My schedule's too full. Can you do it?"

During this conversation, Mrs. Boehm had been passing back and forth, serving breakfast and clearing used dishes. Now she paused in the kitchen doorway and cleared her throat.

"No need agency," she announced. "Know someone."

"You do?" said Griffith with relief. "Who?"

"Is he good? Professional?" asked Jessica cautiously.

Mrs. Boehm nodded firmly. "My nephew Ramon. Sister Olga's boy. Very good. He work for Goldschmidt, the banker, three days a week. Could use more work. I tell him?"

"Fine. When can he start?" said Griffith returning to his journal.

Jessica glanced at her husband in annoyance but

she nodded to Mrs. Boehm. "We'll take your recommendation. Have him call me at the clinic—uh—after four today."

So the following Saturday, Ramon Czernak started on the Brainard yard. Barbara was awakened before eight by the sound of the power mower beneath her window. It was the first day of spring vacation. Grumpily she poked her head out to see the gardener's slight, denimed figure moving steadily back and forth across the grass. He never looked around but concentrated on steering the mower in straight lines. As he moved, the lawn became smooth and carpetlike, the clippings collected neatly in a canvas bag attached to the mower. He wasn't a muscular man, but he had no trouble manipulating the heavy mower around corners or carrying the bulky bags of clippings. She could see the muscles move on his neck as he strained to lift the bags.

She sighed. Spring vacation was the time for nice, late sleeping; what good was vacation if you didn't sleep late? Now that she was awake, she might as well get up.

Ramon came in for a drink of water while she was eating her grapefruit. He grinned at Mrs. Boehm and called her Tia Margarethe; when he noticed Barbara, he bowed formally. Mrs. Boehm proudly introduced him. Barbara held out her hand; he took it, bowed again and kissed her fingers. She looked into his dark brown eyes and fell instantly in love.

He was only about four inches taller than she was; his hair curled over his ears and he had a cleft in his chin that entranced her. Constantly she pestered Mrs. Boehm for information about him. It wasn't difficult. The housekeeper loved to chat about her relatives. Ramon's mother was sister Olga Czernak; the other sister was Elsa Ferris, mother of someone in Barbara's class, whom Barbara hadn't yet recognized.

However she listened intently as Mrs. Boehm told her the story of how she, Henry, her husband, Elsa and Olga, with her husband George and infant Ramon, had escaped from Hungary. It sounded like a movie: the terror, the tension, the need for secrecy; the desperation that forced a family to abandon friends and property to try for life in an unknown land where only George spoke the language. She looked at Mrs. Boehm's short, stocky figure in its crisp cotton print with the lace on the pockets and at the neck. It was difficult to see a younger, slimmer woman running through the night, covering the nephew's mouth to prevent an audible whimper from betraying the group.

Ramon remembered nothing of the escape. He told Barbara he was too young and, furthermore, he wasn't interested. What was past was past. He was friendly and courteous to her, while she discovered an interest in gardening of which her parents had been unaware.

She breakfasted early every morning in order to be at the table when Ramon arrived for work. He only came on Tuesdays, Thursdays and Saturdays, but on the days he didn't work, she found ways to get Mrs. Boehm to talk about him, what he liked to do, to eat, his ambition to be a landscape architect.

"Pah!" said Mrs. Boehm at that. "A doctor he should be. Make money."

"What if he doesn't want to?" said Barbara. Her parents wanted her to be a doctor, too. She could sympathize. Being a doctor wasn't so great. Your time was never your own; your family couldn't count on you for holidays. She'd never be a doctor.

"What he know?" said Mrs. Boehm, waving a feather duster. "He a kid."

"He's nineteen," said Barbara defiantly. To her that seemed, if not old, at least adult.

"Alla same." Mrs. Boehm set her chin and began to dust vigorously. The subject was closed. Sighing, Barbara picked up her book. If Mrs. Boehm wouldn't discuss something, that was that.

But she discovered other ways to learn about Ramon. On Wednesdays, after a quick whisking through the house, Mrs. Boehm went grocery shopping. If she was home, Barbara went with her. She always enjoyed any shopping and sometimes they stopped at sister Olga's for tea. Ramon wouldn't be there, but there was a photograph of him on an end table, a candid shot that showed him, shirt open at the neck, hair mussed in the wind, that Barbara could dream about. And Olga Czernak loved to talk about her only son. Sometimes, Mrs. Boehm accused her of boasting, but Olga retorted that she was just jealous since she had no children of her own. Often the women lapsed into Hungarian, which Barbara couldn't understand, but she didn't care. It gave her a chance to look at Ramon's picture and plan a way to make him notice her, maybe even someday he would kiss her hand again.

Once, sister Elsa also stopped in for tea. Barbara learned that the one who was in Room 100 was Virgil Ferris. She pretended to recognize the name, but the only Ferris in the class was Ned, she knew. Who on earth was Virgil Ferris? Most likely Margery would know.

She did. "Sure. That's Ned," she said casually the next day.

"How do you know?" asked Barbara. "No one ever calls him Virgil, not even Miss McNealy."

"They'd better not. He hates it. But it's the official name on his records. I work in the office, remember. I saw his permanent record card." She grinned at Barbara. "No, I don't remember—or look up everyone's grades or I.Q.'s. I'm not supposed to talk about them either."

As Margery spoke, Ned passed them on his bike. He waved briefly and whistled by way of greeting. Barbara stared after his rapidly retreating figure.

"Where's he off to in such a hurry," she wondered aloud. "He used to talk with us sometimes."

Margery shrugged. "Ned's got a couple of jobs. He's the morning paper boy, and I heard that he just got a job delivering the weekly afternoon *Sentinel*. He also retrieves lost grocery carts, I think." She laughed and sighed a little. "I wish I could earn the way he does. But he's got a lot of brothers and sisters—seven anyway—and he earns all his spending money and most of his clothes."

Barbara looked after Ned, now disappearing in

the distance, with renewed respect. How awful to have to actually work for money, she thought. Of course, she would be doing it someday, but that was still far in the future, after college. So far she had always been given whatever she needed and most of what she wanted. The need to earn had never been uppermost; it had been the same for her classmates in the private school in California. For all of her life, the necessities, even luxuries, had been provided without thought on her part. But now, here was Ned who held not one but at least two part-time jobs. He kept his schoolwork up, too. It was certainly food for thought.

So, after she left Margery, when she saw a grocery cart abandoned behind some bushes and others in a vacant lot, she took notice and told Ned the next morning. He nodded briskly when she asked if he was interested.

"Sure thing. I get two bucks for every one I bring back. Where are they?"

"Uh—in the bushes on Elm—those tall ones just past the church, I think." She paused. "No—on this side of the church. There's two others in the gully of the vacant lot on our corner, too."

"Wow! Three!" His eyes brightened. "With what I have saved up, that'll give me enough to get a pair of shoes." He held up a foot and showed Barbara the hole in the sole." Then he frowned. "The only trouble is, it's a problem to get three carts back to the store at once. I don't suppose you noticed whether they came from the same store?"

She shook her head. "No, I couldn't tell. But, if you'll meet me at the corner, I'll show you where they are and help you get them back."

"Hey! That'd be great." He hesitated a moment. "I could cut you in for part of the money."

"Don't be silly. It's your job. They wouldn't give me any money for them. They'd probably accuse me of stealing the carts in the first place," she said firmly. "I don't mind helping. I wasn't doing anything much Saturday anyway."

WHEN BARBARA WOKE on Saturday morning, the rain was drizzling gently down her windows. She wasn't surprised; it had rained for twenty-eight of the past thirty days. She put on plastic boots, scarf and raincoat and sloshed down to the corner to meet Ned. Measle watched her go; he was sitting in the bedroom window, kneading his toes and watching the rain sprinkling the window and appearing to wonder who in his right mind would go out on a day like this.

She wondered that herself as moisture crept down the back of her neck, but a promise was a promise. Ned was on time. He didn't appear to relish wandering around in the rain either. They found the three carts without much trouble, although he got pretty muddy struggling in the depths of the bushes. Then they found two other carts behind the Sunday school building. Ned was ecstatic.

"Boy!" he chortled as they pushed the nested carts down Elm Street. "I can sure use the money." But when he tucked the bills into his pocket, he said diffidently, "Are you sure you won't take some of this?" When she shook her head firmly, he added, "Then the least I can do is buy you a Coke."

She felt self-conscious as she perched on a stool at The Hut and stirred her lemon Coke with a straw. It was the first time a boy had ever bought her anything, or gone anywhere with her alone. This might be classed as a date, almost, mightn't it? He wasn't Rhett Butler, or even Ramon but still. . . . She peered at Ned out of the corner of her eye. He was looking at the contents of his glass with intense concentration; she was suddenly aware that he was embarrassed as she was. The idea made her chuckle.

"What's so funny?" he asked.

"Oh, nothing. I was—ah—just thinking what a strange way to spend a Saturday morning," she said. "I never expected to go wallowing around in the mud and wet. I think I'm related to our cat. He doesn't like to get wet either."

Ned laughed, relaxed and began to talk about what he was saving the money for. If he wanted college, he would need to earn all the money.

"Ramon—he's my cousin—could go here to the University practically free. His father is an instructor there. But—can you imagine—he isn't sure he wants to go."

"He doesn't? Why not?" Evidently Ned didn't know that Ramon worked for the Brainards; he probably didn't know that his aunt was their housekeeper either. She felt shy about mentioning it, as if she were bragging.

"Dunno." Ned shrugged. "He just says he's not sure. That he might want to do something else. But I'm going to go. I know I am." His jaw was thrust out determinedly.

"I'm sure you are." She slid off the stool. "I'd better go now. Thank you for the Coke."

"Thanks for the help. I couldn't have brought back five carts without you. I'll walk you back."

Together they left The Hut and walked along Elm Street, heads bent against the rain. It was now coming down steadily. They were about halfway down the block when there was a terrific flash of light, a clap of thunder so loud it hurt her chest, and the sky opened up and the rain came down in buckets, The cloudburst was so heavy, they couldn't see; even in raincoats, they were wet to the skin. When the lightning flashed, Barbara jumped and clutched her ears. She hadn't gotten accustomed to thunderstorms yet; she didn't think she ever would.

"I hate thunder!" she shouted at Ned. "I just hate it." He steered her to a nearby doorway where they huddled for a few minutes.

"It should let up soon," he said. "It never rains this hard for very long." But the wind drove the rain so hard, the doorway was no protection, and it came down even harder. It rushed in sheets across the street and filled the gutters to overflowing.

"C'mon," he said finally, pulling her after him into the storm. "It's not getting any better. We'll go to my house and dry off. It's closer than yours."

The Ferris house was partway down the nearby side street. It stood in the middle of a tiny garden that was beginning to show spring color. Blooming tulips and daffodils lined the front walk. The house was small and shabby; the front porch sagged considerably when they crossed it, but when they opened the front door, a joyous rush of sound met their ears. It was partly due to a loudly playing radio, partly to a practicing violinist somewhere in the back of the house, and partly to a group of voices arguing happily over the dining table. As Barbara and Ned came through the door, everyone stopped talking to stare at them, and a small dog raced over, then stopped short and just looked up at their wetness. One of the children called to the dog and took it away. Barbara did not see it again, nor did anyone mention it. It seemed odd, but she didn't ask.

"Wow, are you wet!" said a boy who turned out to be nine-year-old Byron. "Aren't you smart enough to come in out of the rain?"

Ned ignored him as he introduced Barbara around the table.

"We got pretty wet," he said unnecessarily as they dripped on the braided rug. "I thought maybe she could dry off here—or borrow some clothes."

"Eloise is the only one tall enough," said Elizabeth, looking up at Barbara. She was only a year younger than Byron, but several inches shorter; she wore her dark red hair in short curly ringlets around her head and talked in quick, jerky phrases. She nodded toward the back of the house. "She's practicing—as you can hear."

"Ned, is that you?" called an adult voice. "Did you get very wet?" Before he could answer, the kitchen door opened and Mrs. Boehm's sister, Elsa Ferris, came in, wiping her hands on her apron. She stopped short at the sight of Barbara, wet and bedraggled, beside the table. Ned started to explain, but she smiled and bobbed her head. "Her I already know. She was at Tante Olga's the other day. And I can see that she needs dry clothes. Ach, it's coming down in waterfalls."

Now Barbara had to explain. She felt ill-at-ease and tried to be offhand and casual. But the Ferrises didn't seem concerned.

"I knew Tante Marg was working for a doctor's family," said Ned easily. "I just didn't know it was yours. She says it's a good job." He grinned and began to pull off his boots.

That Saturday afternoon was the most fun Barbara had had since the slumber party. Mrs. Boehm was called and told not to worry. While Ned changed his wet things, Mrs. Ferris found a bathrobe for Barbara to wear; it wrapped around her thin figure nearly twice, and she had to keep holding it closed at the neck. Eloise finished practicing, came into the kitchen and burst into laughter.

"I'll find you a skirt and sweater that ought to fit better than that," she said immediately.

Elizabeth arranged Barbara's wet clothes on one of the registers; they obviously didn't have a dryer. Then they got out a battered Monopoly game. Barbara had never played before, and she soon found she was no match for any of them, especially Byron, the family champ. "He'll be a millionaire, that one, before he's thirty," said Mrs. Ferris with pride.

Emily, the youngest, went broke as soon as Barbara did; she slid from her chair and laid a timid hand on Barbara's arm.

"Would you read to me, please?" Her eyes were

enormous in her pale face. Barbara thought she looked delicate enough to blow away in the first breeze. She mustn't get outside very much, and she was so thin. She noticed that the rest of the family treated Emily as if she were made of bone china. They listened carefully when she talked—or rather whispered—and sometimes their eyes would follow her around the room. But Emily seemed unaware of any extra attention. She stood patiently waiting for Barbara to answer.

"Sure, I'll read to you. What do you have?"

It was *Paddington Bear* and, while the game progressed through several noisy arguments, Barbara and Emily enjoyed the adventures of the small bear from Peru. It was not the first time Emily had heard the story, Barbara found; when she accidentally skipped a sentence, Emily gently corrected her.

"Can you read?" asked Barbara. Emily was only four, but still some children learned to read that early.

The little girl shook her head. "No, only a few words. But I know all my stories by heart."

Barbara stayed for dinner and discovered that sister Elsa was as good a cook as Mrs. Boehm. The girls took over the clean-up duties, so Barbara pitched in, too. She hadn't ever actually washed dishes before, but it turned out to be fun, with everyone joking and teasing. The girls wanted to know what it was like to be an only child, and Barbara could only think how lonely she often was. By this time, her clothes were dry. She changed; Ned was delegated to walk her home, and they were soon picking their way down the soggy streets.

"Ned, can I ask you something?" she said after a period of silent walking.

"Depends. Maybe."

"Is Emily sick or something? She's so pale and she took medicine when she ate."

He hesitated a long time. Barbara began to think he wasn't going to answer when he sighed and said soberly, "She's as healthy as she'll ever be, I guess. We don't talk about it much, but she—she has epilepsy."

"Oh—I'm sorry."

He nodded and kept on walking, his head bent, his hands shoved in his jacket pockets. "She doesn't have convulsions as long as she takes her medication. But we watch her—I suppose you noticed."

After a while, he continued to talk. "I've known for a year or more. Before that I guess I was too young. She had a couple of seizures before Tante Marg talked Mom and Dad into taking her to a doctor. That was before we moved here."

"I—I see. Did the doctor help?"

"It took a while. He tried different stuff. He didn't seem very sure. That's the main reason I'm going to college. I want to go into research—to find out why these things happen."

"There isn't anything to be done?"

"I guess not." They walked awhile without talking, then he burst out. "It's so unfair! She never did anything to deserve that. She's a good kid. Why did it happen to her?"

Barbara had no answer. She remembered Emily's

calmly taking her pill before dinner. What did she think of her illness? At four, how much was she aware of it? What was a seizure like? Barbara sighed. She had always enjoyed good health; in fact, she had never even known anyone with a physical handicap, at all. She resolved to ask her parents, when she had a chance, about epilepsy.

Neither of her parents was home when she got there; the double garage gaped blackly open.

"Come on in, Ned. Maybe Mrs. Boehm'll give us something to eat," she offered. "I could do with a snack."

Mrs. Boehm came bustling out of the kitchen, wiping her hands on her apron. She still had a smudge of flour on her cheek when she opened the front door.

"Ach, I'm glad you home, Barbara. Bad storm, nein? Maybe soon no electricity. I bake retes. Come, you, too, Virgil." She turned back toward the kitchen.

"See. I knew she'd have something to eat." Barbara glanced at Ned and was surprised to see him turn the color of his hair; then she remembered that he didn't know she knew his real name. "Come on in. Let's ask for hot chocolate, too. I already knew your name. So does Margery, as a matter of fact."

"I might have known," he mumbled, following her down the hall. "Nothing's sacred around here."

It was comfortable in the kitchen. Ned and Barbara perched on stools, drank hot chocolate, ate flaky, cherry retes and teased Mrs. Boehm. Barbara felt she knew both the housekeeper and the nephew far better than before this day.

[nine]

THE FOLLOWING MONDAY was bright and sunny. Rain had washed the streets as well as trees and bushes; the landscape looked clean and shiny. Warm breezes from the south gave a definite promise of the spring and summer to come. Barbara happily left her down jacket and boots in the closet. When she left for school, she found Measle sitting hopefully beneath the bird feeder. He ignored her stroking and kept his emerald eyes firmly fixed on the swinging container. The sparrows ignored the cat as they scrapped and flung seeds in all directions. She noticed, however, that they did keep beady eyes on him and stay a safe distance away.

With a light heart, Barbara headed for school. She was involved in the end of school pageant about Japan and was anxious to see what the class thought of the poetry she had written. Also, she was helping Margery put finishing touches on the class play. School was fun. It wouldn't even matter that her old nickname had surfaced.

"Hi, Ned, Edward," she said cheerfully as she dropped her math book on the table. "I solved problem twenty-two."

Edward grinned and patted himself awkwardly on the back. "That's 'cause I'm a great teacher," he said. Barbara stuck her tongue out at him. Ned smiled halfheartedly; he seemed to be engrossed in his work. Before she could say anything further, Florence arrived with a request for help with scene painting for the pageant. The day moved smoothly along; although occasionally Barbara glanced at Ned. He appeared to be unusually preoccupied all day. At lunch she asked Margery about it.

"I noticed," said Margery frowning. "But I don't know why. I hope it isn't anything wrong with Emily." She crumpled up her sandwich bag and stood up. "There he goes now. Let's ask."

They disposed of their trash and followed Ned down the hall. He moved slowly, his shoulders hunched.

"Hey, Ned," called Barbara, "wait up." He halted obediently; but when they came closer, Barbara saw that his face was strained and closed.

"Why're you so glum today?" asked Barbara. She saw no reason to beat around the bush. "Didn't you get problem twenty-two?"

"Twenty-two? What . . . oh, that," he said and relaxed a little. "I did it yesterday."

"Then what's wrong?" said Margery persistently. "Is it Emily? You haven't been yourself all morning."

"No—o," said Ned slowly. "Not directly, but sort of. . . ."

"Ned Ferris, what is it?" said Barbara. She wanted to shake him in exasperation.

"It's—it's Choto—the dog. You saw her, when you were over, Barbara." She remembered the small bundle of wriggling fur. "Emily's allergic to her and we have to get rid of her—Choto—not Emily." He managed a small smile. "We were keeping her outside, thinking that would help. But after all the rain on Saturday, we decided that wasn't practical. So now she has to go."

"Gee, I'm sorry," said Margery soberly. "What'll you do?"

He shook his head. "I don't know. Give her to someone, I guess. I hope anyway. I can't stand it if we have to take her to the pound."

"You won't," said Margery optimistically. "Someone will give her a home. She's a cute little dog."

"Why don't you take her?" said Ned hopefully. He shoved his hands in his pockets and wet his lips. "She doesn't take up much space."

"Gee, I'd like to, but we can't have pets. The landlord's so strict, we can't even have a parakeet."

"How about me?" said Barbara suddenly. "I'll take her." She had been thinking rapidly as Ned explained his preoccupation. She had wanted a dog for a long time—for years, in fact. Everyone had said she was too young, but now she wasn't. She felt much older. A small dog like Choto wouldn't be much work. Her parents would probably leave it up to Mrs.

Boehm; they wouldn't want to upset the housekeeper unnecessarily. But how could Mrs. Boehm object, if by taking Choto it would help Ned and his family? She shifted her books and said again more positively, "I'll take Choto. We have a nice yard for a dog."

"Brains, can you? That's great," said Ned. He brightened considerably. "That's just great. When can you get her?"

"You also have a cat," said Margery. "What about Measle?"

"He'll be okay. He's bigger than she is, and anyway a lot of dogs and cats live together." Barbara spoke more positively than she felt, but she couldn't take it back now after seeing the expression in Ned's eyes. "I'll come by after school and get her, if that's okay."

It was a long afternoon for Barbara. Worries scurried around in her head like squirrels in a cage. She had wanted to have a dog; now she had one. Did she know enough about dog care? How much would Choto eat? What did she eat? How could she—Barbara—make Measle love Choto? How could anyone make anyone love anyone else? Mrs. Boehm probably would be all right; likely so would her parents. Still . . . here she was being impulsive again. Would she ever learn? But there was Ned looking cheerful. He even said he hoped they could come visit Choto once in a while. That was worth a lot of trouble.

Instead of turning down her own street, after school, Barbara waved goodbye to Margery and continued with Ned to the little brown house.

Ned's brothers and sisters had arrived earlier and

were surprised to see Barbara and pleased. Emily came from the baby-sitter next door and asked for a story.

"She can't stay," said Ned carefully. "She came for Choto."

"Choto!" chorused the voices.

Everyone was aware of the need to find a home for the dog. She had been a gift from the neighbor whose dog had the litter, and even though they had only had her a few months, she was greatly loved. However, it was obviously necessary.

Eloise begin to list food requirements while Byron searched for the dog dishes and leash. As if aware of her new mistress, Choto sat on Barbara's feet and licked her ankles. When Barbara bent to scratch the dog's neck, the dog lifted her head and peered through the fringe of hair that hung over her bright brown eyes. She seemed to be searching for reassurance, and Barbara was torn between pleasure at having a dog, and sorrow at seeing the Ferris children's unhappiness; there was also concern about how she would explain things at home.

Within a short time, Barbara waved goodbye and headed down the street, clutching her books and restraining Choto, who bounced exuberantly at the end of the leash. Evidently a walk to anywhere was a rare treat.

As she drew nearer home, Barbara's steps slowed; in her mind she tried to form words to explain to Mrs. Boehm, but somehow now it wasn't so easy. She wished she'd asked Ned to come along. In spite of her slow pace, eventually she did arrive home. And both her parents' cars stood in the drive.

"Oh, lord!" she groaned aloud. She had forgotten today was Thursday and they often were home for an early dinner. Now she had to face the three of them at once. Ugh! She braced her shoulders and opened the front door.

"Hi, Mom! Hi, Dad," she said brightly, ignoring the leash in her hand. "How're things?"

"Hello, Barb." Griffith didn't turn from his crouched position in front of the fireplace. "How was school?"

Jessica waved a hand and began to speak before she looked around. "Hi, Barb. We thought we'd have a fire to—" She stopped speaking and stared at Choto. At her silence, Griffith stood up and he, too, stared at the small dog.

"Ah—I guess you wonder," said Barbara tentatively. "That is . . . how I . . . I can't very well say she followed me home, can I?" She unsnapped the leash.

"No, I don't think you can," said Jessica evenly.

"Her name's Choto. She belonged to Ferrises, but they couldn't keep her. Emily's allergic to dog hair, and it's brought on a couple seizures. So they had to find a home. Margery couldn't because of the landlord. So there was only me—I?—And I've always wanted a dog. . . . And—and you wouldn't let a cute dog like this go to the pound, would you?" she finished lamely.

"You mean in all of Berea, you were the only

human being who could offer a home to—to this?" said her father skeptically.

"Well—maybe not," she admitted honestly, but the Ferrises can visit her here, so it's almost like not having to give her up. And isn't she darling?" She stooped to pat the little dog, who had retreated to between Barbara's feet.

"I think she's cute," said Jessica doubtfully. "But which way is she facing?"

"What kind of dog is she—you said she?" said Griffith. He hadn't tried to pat Choto, but he wasn't frowning either. That was a good sign. Her mother, also, looked reserved but not cold or aloof.

"I don't know," said Barbara, "except her name's Choto."

"She looks like a lhasa apso," said Jessica. She held out her hand to Choto, who sniffed cautiously. "Is she spayed?"

At least Barbara knew that. "Eloise said she is. She's not quite a year. Is—is it all right?" She held her breath. "I can keep her, can't I?"

Shrugging, Griffith threw a log on the fire and brushed his hands. "What do you say, Jess? Okay with you?"

She stroked Choto's ears and stood up. "Maybe. But, Barb, you know it depends on Mrs. Boehm. I won't have her upset. And the care will be absolutely up to you."

"I know, Mom. I'll do it, really I will. Look." She held out the bowls and a small bag of dog food Eloise had thoughtfully provided. "Here's enough food for a couple days, until we can get to a store."

Before Jessica could comment, Mrs. Boehm appeared in the doorway. Wiping her hands on her apron, she bobbed her head in greeting.

"Dr. Brainard, Miz Brainard, what time you—" She stopped talking to stare at the dog. "Why that looks like Choto."

"It is Choto," said Barbara speaking very fast. "Ned said Emily's allergic, and they had to find a home. I said we'd take her. That way the kids can visit her sometimes. She's very small and no trouble. I'll take care of her—every day. Isn't she adorable? You don't mind, do you?"

"I guess." The housekeeper tilted her head to one side as she considered. "I no mind. I like dogs. And anyway"—she pointed a finger at Barbara—"you feed. I see to it."

"Now all you've got to worry about is Measle," said Griffith grinning.

"That's settled," said Jessica briskly. "Now, when's dinner?"

Dinner was ready in half an hour. Barbara followed her parents into the dining room where she set the puppy on the floor beside her chair. Choto promptly curled up on her feet and stayed there. As they were eating desert, Measle peered cautiously around the corner, but he didn't come any closer.

Barbara watched him out of the corners of her eyes, holding her breath. He moved silently across the room, passing close to Barbara's chair. The puppy lifted her head and peered in Measlo's direction. Curious, she stood up and raised her head to sniff. The two animals were only inches apart. The pup sniffed

145

again, coming even closer. Instantly, Measle administered a sharp slap across Choto's nose.

"Yipe!" squeaked the dog, retreating behind Barbara's feet. With dignity unimpaired, Measle strolled to the kitchen, where Mrs. Boehm crooned sympathy, stroked the ruffled fur and, best of all, set out a piece of fresh liver.

Griffith chuckled as Barbara bent to soothe the pup.

"Well, Measle met the newcomer, and they both survived."

"Are you going to keep the name Choto?" asked Jessica grinning.

"I don't know." She ate a little and peeked at the dog still hiding under her chair. "I'll have to think about it." She smiled. "I can hardly believe it. I really have a dog. We really are going to keep her."

Jessica still smiled but said seriously, "But you'll be expected to care for her, train her, all that. It's a big responsibility, and you're not to leave it to Mrs. Boehm. She has enough to do."

"Oh, I will—I won't. I'll take good care of her," said Barbara firmly.

To prove her sincerity, as soon as dinner ended, she found a sturdy cardboard box in the garage, padded it with three worn-out towels and put it beside her bed. She lifted the dog into it when she was ready to retire.

Choto peered at her intently through the fringe, apparently assessing the situation, then evidently decided that this was to be her place, for she curled up in a tight circle, gave a great sigh and appeared to fall instantly asleep.

Later, after all was quiet, as Barbara lay awake watching the moonlight stream through the curtains, she felt a thump beside her pillow. Measle moved like a shadow through the dim light to the foot of the bed; after a thorough grooming, he, too, curled up and slept. Barbara sighed with relief. If Measle had been too upset about the dog, she would have felt terrible. Now all was well. She turned over and was also soon sound asleep.

The next morning she reported to Ned that all was well with Choto. He reminded her of her offer to let Choto visit.

"Sure, but what about Emily? Wouldn't it bother her?"

He shook his head. "It doesn't so much when we're all out of doors."

"Well then, how about Saturday?"

They left it at that. Barbara didn't have time to think much about Choto during the day. She had French homework and play preparations to work on. Afterward, strolling home with Ned and Margery in the late afternoon sunshine, they began to speak of summer plans.

"I still don't understand Edward," said Barbara. Imagine giving up Saturday mornings and part of the summer to learn a computer language." Edward's father, a computer specialist, was offering to teach Basic to anyone interested enough to be at his home by eight a.m. every Saturday morning.

"I am for one," said Margery calmly.

"Whatever for?" said Barbara amazed. "You're good in English. I thought you'd major in that."

"No—at least not completely." Margery shook her head. "I need a way to earn my living as soon as I graduate from high school. Knowing a computer language will be a big help. Maybe I'll get to college. I'm certainly going to try. But it'll take a scholarship, a job and a whole lot of luck."

"For me, too," said Ned. He stripped a privet leaf from a hedge, and as they walked, he creased it and then tore it into very small pieces. "Besides, a knowledge of computers is the coming thing. Edward says it isn't difficult to learn. So why not? Who knows when it'll come in handy. But how about you, Brains? Are you taking a trip this summer?"

She shook her head. "Don't know. Usually I get sent to summer camp. My parents are always too busy to take a trip, except for medical conventions. In fact, the move from San Diego was the first time the three of us have ever traveled together." It was a little off-putting, she thought, that while both Ned and Margery accepted responsibilities for themselves, they assumed she would spend the summer playing. The trouble was, they were probably right. She had figured on a leisurely summer. But now, it didn't seem like such a lot of fun. Perhaps she could do something, accomplish something.

"Maybe I'll take that special French class at the college," she said at last. "Miss Chessin thought it would help me catch up so I could be in advanced French with you next fall in junior high."

When Miss Chessin had proposed it, Barbara had had no intention of signing up; now, however, she began to think of summer school with enthusiasm. Maybe it was time she did some growing up. A person could play just so much.

"Great," said Margery. "Why don't we plan to have lunch together everyday. I'll be learning business machines at the high school next door."

"And I'm taking chemistry."

"You can't take that, Ned. You're not old enough," said Barbara.

He grinned. "Yes, I can. They have a credit class for Majors. If I do all right, it'll give me three units of high school science."

"It's one of the times it helps to be smart," said Margery. "I'm going to try to finish high school in two and a half years by going to summer school."

"You won't have any fun at all this summer."

"Yes, we will. We'll have afternoons. That's plenty of time. And we can have lunch together."

As she waved goodbye, she called to Ned, "Don't forget about Saturday." He waved his math book to show he had heard.

So the following Saturday afternoon, after computer class, Barbara attached a leash to Choto and walked briskly along Elm to meet the Ferris children. Choto bounced along happily, first pulling to the left and then to the right, then behind Barbara, tangling her legs. The two groups met halfway down the block. The children rushed toward her, scaring Choto so that she hid behind Barbara's legs. Then perhaps she remembered, for she bounced out and into their midst, panting and wagging and wriggling all over. Barbara stood to one side and watched, feeling warm and happy; she had never before had the experience of bringing so much pleasure to anyone. Even small Emily knelt and tentatively stroked Choto's squirming back. She breathed a little faster, but otherwise seemed to show no ill effects. The children walked back to the Brainard house and spent a short, happy hour.

But at last Ned stood back from the group. "Okay, kids. We gotta go. I've got collections to make, and Emily has to take her medicine."

Reluctantly the others gathered together, looking longingly at Choto. Barbara held Choto's collar. The little dog pulled after the children as they straggled behind Ned; Frank and William walked backwards until they fell over a tree root.

"You can come see her anytime," Barbara called after them. Eloise waved to show she heard.

That night at dinner Barbara asked her mother about epilepsy and allergy.

Jessica shook her head. "It's your father's specialty, not mine."

"Why do you want to know, Barb?" he asked curiously. "You've never shown any interest in my work before."

She explained about Emily. He sighed, looking sober.

"It's a tragic disability at any time; but I think when it strikes during childhood, it's even sadder. Of course, there are medicines that help keep it under control. But unfortunately, added problems like allergies are often present."

"What causes it, Dad?"

He shook his head. "Sometimes trauma—injury —sometimes brain tumors. Sometimes we just don't know."

"If it's a tumor—you could operate, couldn't you?"

He held up a hand. "Don't involve me," he said firmly. "I don't operate on children. Besides, Emily's not my patient. It sounds as if she's in good hands." He smiled at her disappointed expression. "We can't always fix it when something is wrong. But she's lucky to be part of such a caring family."

Barbara agreed with that. There was much about life with the Ferrises that she envied. What would it be like, she wondered, to be one of those children? In *Cheaper by the Dozen*, there were twelve. She'd never be lonely then. That would be certain.

In school, she was continually amazed at the ambition that the kids in Room 100 showed. Instead of trying to get out of work, everyone seemed intent on signing up for as many things as they could handle. Of course, Ned and Margery had solid reasons for wanting the extra studies. Barbara didn't fit in that category, but the more she thought about it, the better the idea seemed. Three months with nothing to do but loaf could be—usually was—very boring. Maybe she'd even turn up for the computer class. Ramon might be impressed with her energy; he still always treated her like a kid. She would bring it up at dinner—if either of her parents was home.

As she expected, they were surprised. "Why, Barb?" said her mother. "Your grades are good enough now. You don't need to make up any work."

"It's just—just that maybe it's time to do something besides play in the summer. I'll be in junior high in the fall and, if I try, I can be in advanced French. I think I like languages." She wound up trying not to sound defensive. "The tuition is kind of expensive but. . . ."

"It probably isn't any more than the cost of camp," said her father slowly. "But that's not the point. Are you sure—"

"I think it's a fine idea," said Jessica briskly. "Camp must be boring by now. French, you said?"

Encouraged, Barbara nodded enthusiastically. "And I think I'll join Edward's computer class. That's free," she added, seeing her father's raised eyebrows. "His father's offering to teach a bunch of us on Saturdays."

"You're planning on a busy summer," said Griffith. "Don't forget your responsibilities—I mean Choto and Measle."

[ten]

However, determination was not accomplishment and Barbara soon began to feel like a new mother. Where her free time had been her own for loafing and hanging around the garden, now there was always something to claim her attention. Of course, there was schoolwork, nowadays not so automatically simple. In addition, Jessica and Mrs. Boehm meant what they said, and she was wakened early, even during weekends, to feed Choto; the dog needed frequent brushing, too, because her soft, silky coat became tangled constantly. Also, she badly needed lessons in leash walking. Then, too, there was Measle to soothe and comfort so that the cat wouldn't feel neglected.

Choto turned out to be a very bright little dog. At first she crept quietly around the house, cringing whenever the cat came into the room. But as the days passed, she began to bounce as she walked, and she made the first tentative overtures to Measle. The cat seemed to feel that he had made his point with the first slap, to assume there was no need for any further demonstration. After a while, however, even he accepted Choto's exuberance with equanimity. He went out of his way to brush past her when he came into the house, and one day Barbara found them sleeping side by side in Choto's bed. Rather than feeling neglected, Measle had, like any cat, found the warmest, most comfortable spot available. Barbara began to feel like Dr. Doolittle.

In addition to the pets, there were the Saturday lessons at Edward's. He and his father had built a mini-computer from a kit; for his science project next year, Edward said he was planning to design a database management program. His father was chief programmer for the auto plant. They were both ordinarily quiet and self-contained people; but when talking computers their eyes sparkled and they showed genuine animation. Then Edward was a totally different person from the boy Barbara knew from Room 100.

Their obsession seemed weird to her. What was there about a science fiction version of a typewriter that was so great? Whenever a person relied on it, the screen suddenly went blank or it flashed something annoying like, SYNTAX ERROR or ARE YOU SURE—CAN'T FIND. How ridiculous. By the time she figured out which buttons to press, she could have done it herself without the computer.

But then she ran a successful program, and the machine flashed WELL DONE. What a triumph! You couldn't fool a computer. It was terrific! She could hardly wait for next Saturday. Maybe she'd read H. G. Wells next.

She tried, unsuccessfully, to tell Mrs. Boehm and then Ramon how much fun it was. Mrs. Boehm merely smiled, nodded and said, "Fine. Have fun." Then she handed Barbara the folded laundry to put away.

Later, while Ramon fertilized the roses, she explained the feeling of success she had. Ramon wasn't even as interested as his aunt. He merely scratched his head, smiled and shrugged.

"It's a lot of nonsense," he said digging away furiously with the cultivator.

"No, it isn't. Ramon. Everything's done with computers these days."

"I don't see none working around these roses." He straightened his back and used his handkerchief to wipe sweat off his face. "Computers may be okay in their way," he said, "but I don't have no use of 'em." He smiled enchantingly at her and went back to cultivation.

Barbara gave up. Ramon was still her hero—sort of—but he certainly had limited interests. She went inside to find either Choto or Measle. She could pet the cat and listen to him purr or play fetch with the dog. They were lying side by side in a patch of spring sunshine. Occasionally Choto reached out with a small pink tongue to wash the cat's ear. Measle accepted this attention tolerantly; Barbara suspected he might even enjoy it.

She sprawled out beside them on the rug. Measle regarded her steadily, his pupils narrow slits in the emerald eyes. Choto peered through her fringe and wagged a curly tail happily.

"I know you don't understand," she told them, "but at least you listen."

Margery, too, listened and agreed. She was as fascinated by computers as Barbara. Later that afternoon they sat on Barbara's back porch eating brownies, Ramon came by trundling a wheelbarrow loaded with peat moss. His shirt was open halfway down, showing tanned skin and bulging muscles. He grinned at the girls and moved away.

Barbara sighed. "Isn't he dreamy?" she said.

"Who? Oh, Ramon?" said Margery surprised. She shrugged. "Sure, he's handsome, sort of. Not my type, though. And he's going to get married."

A dream crashed in silent tinkles like a Christmas ornament for Barbara. "But—he's only nineteen. He isn't going to marry. Mrs. Boehm's his aunt and she says he's going to be a landscape architect."

"She doesn't know everything," said Margery grimly. "He's dating my sister, Shirley, and they're planning on marriage by November at the latest." Her face twisted with disgust. "They're both stupid. I don't know why they're so stupid, but they are."

"Well-ll, maybe they're in love."

"Love!" Her tone made it sound obscene. "Will love pay the rent? Will it be enough when boredom sets in? When Shirley's thirty-five and losing her looks and he takes after a waitress?"

"He—he won't. At least he might not. You can't tell."

Margery raised her eyebrows. "Who says? Statistics don't agree with you." She bit into another brownie. "I want more than that for myself. Shirley should have higher goals."

"You're not going to get married?"

"Oh, sure—maybe—eventually. But there's a lot I want to do first." The girls ate and watched Ramon work for a few minutes; then Margery began to talk.

"Brains, you don't know what it's like to have two older sisters, to see what they're doing with their lives. Shirley's only seventeen. She works part-time at The Hut and saves every cent for her trousseau." Again her face twisted with revulsion. "She works and scrimps, and it'll never be any different. She and Ramon are planning to be married after she graduates from high school and saves up five hundred dollars." She sighed. "Then there's Dulcie. She's twenty, married and divorced. Her baby's two and a half. She got married the day after she graduated, so when her husband—the rat—walked out, all she could do is be a waitress. The baby was six weeks old when he left."

"Waitresses make pretty good money, I heard, if you count tips," said Barbara. It seemed necessary to defend love and marriage for some reason.

"Sure, for herself it would be fine, but she has to live in an apartment that takes kids. That's an extra fifty bucks a month. And the baby-sitter charges a hundred twenty-five a month and, boy, it better be on time."

"Wow!" said Barbara softly.

"Yeah, wow. Think what she could do with one hundred twenty-five dollars to spend each month. She can't afford the extra sitter fees to go to night school

157

to learn a better paying skill either. Though I must admit," she added honestly, "she probably wouldn't go. Dulcie never was a student. She sort of lets life happen to her."

It was Barbara's turn to sigh. "I guess maybe I'm a drifter, too. I've never thought about it before."

"That's because you never needed to. College is automatic for you, isn't it?" Barbara nodded soberly. "Well, you see, for me it isn't. I'll have to fight for it. But I stand back and see what a mess my sisters have made of their lives—and they're not even twenty-five yet—and I want—I'll have better than that." She banged her fist on the porch railing. "I can't afford to drift along and hope some nice kid, like Ramon, will want to marry me. And I won't take the chance of making someone else responsible for my life. If I'm smart enough to be gifted, I ought to be smart enough to do that for myself."

"That's right, Margery. You smart kid," said Mrs. Boehm. She held a frosty pitcher of lemonade and was smiling broadly. To her the girls looked young and carefree, and she had only overheard the last sentence. They laughed and held out their glasses.

WITH ALL of the various activities, it seemed only a few days until it was the last week of school. The Japanese pageant was presented to the school body on the next to the last day. It was part of the sixth grade graduation ceremonies, but, in the case of Room 100, the fourth and fifth grade took part, too.

Kim Murakami was mistress of ceremonies, even though she was only a fifth-grader. She wore her mother's dress kimono of dainty pink silk with a fiery dragon of red, black and gold thread snaking its way up the back and with a tongue of flame curling over one shoulder. Barbara read some of her haiku standing against the background of delicate, rosy, crepe paper cherry blossoms that had been hand-tied to bare branches, and carefully lettered Japanese signs. The entire class had worked on the signs, and they each had parts in the pantomime that Margery and Barbara had written.

Standing in the wings and peeking, with the others, through a crack in the curtain, Barbara saw her mother. Jessica had said she would try to make it. She had said that before. But this was the first time she had ever managed it. It was very surprising, thought Barbara, but then, after the terrible time when she took the car, her parents had really been making an effort to give her time. Life was really smoothing out, like a novel almost.

Though Jessica sat at the back, her tall, elegant figure stood out clearly. Later, as the parents, mostly mothers, moved around the auditorium chatting and nibbling refreshments, Barbara wished Jessica looked less like a fashion plate and more like a mother. Only her hands with their lack of polish and short trimmed nails were an indication of her profession. The other women were on a first-name basis with each other. Jessica they greeted respectfully as Dr. Brainard. Barbara couldn't tell if she noticed the difference, or if she did, if it bothered her.

Miss McNealy was the sole exception. She put a hand on her shoulder, saying firmly, "Barbara, you must introduce me to your mother."

She stumbled and mumbled the names. It was such nonsense, they knew who they were. She thought, too, that they made an odd picture; stocky Miss McNealy barely five feet tall, with short, curly, red-going-gray hair and Dr. Jessica Brainard, five feet ten with long dark hair in a smooth coil around her head.

But the teacher didn't seem at all intimidated. She grinned easily and said, "How are you finding our community? A big change from southern California, I expect."

Jessica laughed. "Especially the winter."

"Yes, well. . . ." The conversation flowed easily. Barbara stood between them, ignored as is usual when teachers talk with parents. She didn't mind; it left her free to dream about being Eleanor of Aquitaine. She suddenly heard Miss McNealy say, "I'd have known you were Barbara's mother. She's going to look just like you in a few years.

Jessica smiled, patted Barbara's shoulder and said she could see the resemblance, too. Now what did they mean by that? Barbara had often wished that she looked like her mother, graceful and beautifully groomed; but she doubted that it would ever be so. She usually felt groomed by grab bag. Miss McNealy was just trying to be pleasant to a parent, probably.

Later, driving home, Jessica remarked that the pageant was very nicely done.

"You kids did a fine job," she said. "I wouldn't have thought such a small class could be so disciplined."

"Thanks." Barbara leaned back relaxing and thinking, now that it was over, she was pretty tired. "I guess it's because of Miss M."

"She said she was pleased to have had you in her class."

"It's been a good semester. I wish it wasn't over —almost." She chuckled a little. "I'm almost glad I punched Herbie in the stomach that day—that's why I was put in the Majors."

"You what?" gasped Jessica. "No—never mind now. I think I'd rather not know." She patted Barbara's arm. "But I am pleased. So is your father, that your grades have improved so much. What you really needed was a challenge after all."

It was funny, Barbara thought, taking her school supplies upstairs, how much change could happen in less than a year. She had bounced from class heroine to pariah in Miss Joliet's class; then, when she was put in Room 100, she had been very doubtful that she could stay. Everyone was so accomplished. But it had been a wonderful challenge, and she had succeeded. She guessed maybe she did have a good mind, after all. She had really meant it when she said she was almost sorry to have it end.

These last few days had been almost better than fiction. Jo March must have felt this way when she sold her novel. Barbara was torn between being Jo March and Eleanor of Aquitaine.

THERE WAS a bittersweet quality to the final day of school. It was the day toward which everyone had been striving. A short day, it meant the beginning of summer vacation. But it also meant separation for some very good friends; and the fall would mean seventh grade for some of them, with the attendant worries about beginning junior high school. It was one more step in growing up.

The group went to the amusement park at the edge of the long ravine that was Metropolitan Park. Barbara rode on the Rocket five times and discovered that Edward—quiet Edward—liked roller coasters as much as she did. Later, picnicking on the edge of Rocky River, the Kane twins were the only ones who caught any crayfish, in spite of the fact that they all went wading in the icy water and tried very hard, except for Mary Jane who refused to get her feet wet. Everyone was hungry early and glad for Barbara's party.

Mrs. Boehm had a supper of hamburgers ready in the back yard, and for dessert, she had made her marvelously rich Hungarian chocolate cake. They played hide and seek in the twilight until the fireflies came out and began to flit, winking in the gathering darkness. They caught two or three and kept them in a jar while Margery made up stories about captive princesses with signal lights. Kim took the lid off the jar and let the fireflies free. Choto was the center of attention; she danced and wagged happily. Finally, it was time to go in. Mrs. Boehm had dishes of ice cream for everyone and Jessica helped serve.

"Though how you kids can hold any more is beyond me," she said laughing. She had changed into casual denims and a cotton shirt, but she still didn't look motherly, thought Barbara. Jolly Mrs. Boehm was more like a traditional mother, and she didn't have any children. What would it be like if . . . ?

"What's it like, being a surgeon, Dr. Brainard?" asked Kim. "Does it take a long time? Is it hard?"

"It isn't easy," said Jessica, smiling. She talked about the years of medical school, the long hours as an intern and resident. She minimized the worries and frustrations, which Barbara dimly remembered, though she had been small when her mother was a resident.

She finished with a smile and shrug, saying, "So there you have it."

Kim said quietly, "I'm going to be a doctor, too."

Ned and Edward said, "Me, too." They swallowed, blushed and looked at the floor.

Jessica smiled gently and said, "I hope you can, if you really want it enough. It can be fulfilling. It is for me. But sometimes, it's hard on the family." She glanced at Barbara as she spoke, and Barbara smiled back faintly.

And then it was time to go home. They parted full of plans. The younger children were pleased to be a whole grade older—would be at least in the fall. In the meantime, there was a long summer full of games ahead. The sixth—cum seventh—graders were sad to be parting, anxious about a new school, and all eight had summer jobs or classes for which to get ready.

Drifting off to sleep with Measle at her feet and Choto in her basket beside the bed, Barbara thought sleepily that it had been a very successful day, like . . . like the children in *Greengage Summer*. It was becoming harder and harder to find heroines—or heroes—with whom to identify. She wanted to be someone who was beautiful and always successful. It didn't seem to be possible. Everyone always had troubles.

[eleven]

THREE DAYS later Barbara started French class at the college. It was the shortest summer vacation she had ever had, but she made the most of those three days, perhaps because the time was so limited. On one of the afternoons, Ned brought his brothers and sisters to play in the garden with her and with Choto. Mrs. Boehm made a picnic lunch and served it in the rose arbor. The children played hide and seek and sprawled on the grass to feed tidbits to Choto when she danced on her hind legs. It was a merry afternoon, thought Barbara happily, one of many lately. She realized suddenly that she had made more friends in Berea in a few short months than she had in the entire time she had lived in California. In fact, she hardly thought of California at all anymore.

FRENCH CLASS was exciting; it was a thrill just to walk across the campus and to think that she was a part of college life. She wasn't the only kid taking special summer classes; four others from Room 100 were also there. But there were enough genuine college students to make her feel very grown-up, and the setting was right: the great old maples, the manicured lawns, the old brick dormitories. It made her feel part of a never-ending tradition.

Monsieur Picholet was certainly a contrast to Miss Chessin. He was a small, dainty man with the instincts of a tartar.

"Pas d'anglais," he shouted the first morning when someone asked a question in English. He absolutely insisted that only French be spoken at all times. If someone didn't understand in French, they had to find out the answer some other way or risk his frown and low grade underlined in red.

So willy-nilly, they soon became quite facile in the language. Their accents improved, and Barbara even began to think in French.

"Ah, *je suis fatigué,*" she murmured one day as she dropped down on the grass beside Margery and Ned under their favorite maple tree. Ned had a mouthful of peanut butter sandwich and couldn't talk, but Margery could.

"Listen, Brains," she said, "if you're going to go high hat and talk French on us, I'll talk business machines to you." She tossed a potato chip at her.

Barbara dug into her lunch sack laughing. "Sorry. Having to talk French from nine to twelve every day, it gets to be a habit."

"Well, that's the idea, isn't it?" said Ned, swallowing the last of the peanut butter. He pulled out a second sandwich and dubiously surveyed a whole wheat with bits of lettuce peeking between the edges. "I'd know one of Eloise's lunch jobs anywhere. I'll bet it's nothing but lettuce."

"Eloise doesn't pack your lunches," said Margery.

"No. Mom usually does, but she has to fill in for Mrs. Malone at the clinic this week. And we can sure use the money." He glanced at Barbara and said easily, "Mom is on the maintenance crew at the clinic. Usually she works nights, but sometimes she fills in for one of the day women. We manage somehow at home." He began to chew the lettuce sandwich with a noticeable lack of enthusiasm.

Barbara could well imagine they could cope. Everyone in that house had seemed so capable, even little Emily. If the situation called for it, could she, Barbara, handle things as well? Barbara ate her sliced ham and wondered.

"Wow!" said Ned suddenly pointing. "Look at that!"

Both girls turned to see what he was seeing. It was a giant dog, the largest Barbara had ever seen. It roamed aimlessly here and there across the lawn; as students passed, it trotted up to them, sniffing and growling. The dog's head was waist-high to the adults so whenever it approached someone, the person drew back in alarm or shouted, "Go away! Scram!"

"That's a St. Bernard, isn't it?" said Margery doubtfully. "I've never seen a dog that big before."

"Wonder who owns it. Dogs aren't allowed on campus," said Ned.

"Maybe a visitor who doesn't know better." Barbara looked at her watch and stood up. "I'll see you later. There's an afternoon session today." She glanced back over her shoulder at the dog. He was a beautiful animal, with curly brown and white fur and a thick, bushy tail. She hoped he wasn't lost.

The afternoon class was a long one, and the campus was nearly deserted when Barbara started home. Ned was crossing the quad in front of the library pushing his bike. As they came within speaking distance, the St. Bernard rounded the corner of the fountain. Lifting his head, he sniffed at the air and changed direction toward Barbara. As she came close, he stopped on the walk and stood blocking the way. Barbara looked at him; he looked at her and growled.

"Good dog," she said, holding out her hand and speaking soothingly. That was what one did with strange dogs, she knew, but he was awfully large and menacing. And she had to get past him.

"Good dog. Are you lost?" Ned came up beside Barbara; he kicked down the bike stand and reached over to pat the giant head. The dog lifted his muzzle and growled.

"Will he bite?" said Barbara doubtfully.

"Naw, I don't think so. He's probably just growling for effect," said Ned. He ran his hand around the thick fur at the neck. "He doesn't have a collar. I think he's lost."

"How can you lose a St. Bernard?"

"Maybe he's been abandoned. Rotten people do it all the time around here."

"Oh no!" Sympathy made Barbara come close enough to pat the dog. He turned his head toward her and wagged his tail slowly.

"I think he likes you."

"How can you tell?" He was the size of a small bear, and he looked very formidable. She reached out again tentatively. The fur was thick and soft, thicker and deeper than Choto's, though not so soft. She ran her hand down his back and buried it in the thick fur, scratching with her fingers as Choto loved to have her do. Underneath the hide, she could feel the regular line of spinal bones and then the heavy protrusion of pelvic bones. There wasn't much flesh covering them.

"This dog's starving," she gasped. "Feel his back. I'll bet he hasn't eaten in days. No wonder he growls."

Ned felt the thin back and shook his head.

"What can we do?" Barbara looked around desperately. No one was close enough even to shout at. "We can't leave him here."

"No." Ned, too, looked around. "But where . . . I know." He snapped his fingers. "Let's try campus security. They might know if he's lost. Maybe he ran away from someone." He stepped back and clicked his fingers again. "Come on. Here, doggy, doggy. Good dog. Let's go."

He backed away, making coaxing sounds. The dog continued to stand in front of Barbara, motionless except for his heavy breathing. Occasionally he looked at her and wagged his tail gently.

"Brains, you walk this way. I think he's waiting for you," said Ned.

Cautiously, she stepped toward him, around the dog, and sure enough, he lurched after her. They found the security office, and the officer in charge agreed that it was difficult to lose a dog that large. Once he had recovered from the size of the stray, he checked his records. The dog didn't help any by growling loudly whenever the officer made another move.

"No," he said cheerfully as he shut the book. "We have lost beagles and poodles and cockapoos, but no St. Bernards."

"But what should we. . . ." Ned started to say when Barbara began edging out of the office. The great dog lurched along after her.

"Thank you, sir. You'll know where to find us, if you do get a report."

"Why'd you do that," Ned wanted to know when they stood on the sidewalk. "Maybe we could have left him there." The dog leaned against Barbara heavily.

"Sure, and you know what he'd do." Barbara began to walk down the street so fast Ned had to almost trot to keep up. The dog panted heavily alongside them. "He'd phone the pound. And the pound'd keep him for three days and then put him down."

"Maybe they wouldn't." But Ned didn't sound as if he believed himself.

"Sure they would. There's no ID and no proof about rabies shots. They've got more dogs than they can feed now. They don't try to keep unidentified strays." She stopped to talk and the dog bumped into her, almost knocking her down.

"Well, what'll you do?" Ned grinned. "He likes you."

Patiently, the stray watched Barbara, a yard of

pink tongue hanging out of the side of his mouth and his sides heaving as he panted.

"Me?" she gasped. "But . . . why can't you take him?"

Ned shook his head slowly. "I'd sure like to. But remember Emily. If she was allergic to Choto, think how she'd react to a dog this size." He sighed. "We couldn't afford to feed him anyway."

"Well, the only thing is that we have a dog, Choto."

"Yes, but I think he's picked you." He grinned at the dog and then at Barbara.

She looked down and sighed. The dog wagged his tail and panted harder than ever; his tongue lolled off the side of his mouth like a wet towel. Everything about him was so darned big. She grinned reluctantly, thinking of the housekeeper's reaction—or her parents. A dog like this would shake even her mother's composure. Well, maybe they could keep him long enough to find a real home for him.

"Oh dear," she said shaking her head. "I don't see how. . . . There's no leash. . . . And what'll Mrs. Boehm say?"

"I'll bet he'll walk along right beside us." Ned began to rub the dog's head. "I'll come along and explain to Tante Marg. It might not be for long anyway. His real owners'll probably turn up."

"Okay. Come on then." Barbara started off at a brisk pace; she half hoped the huge animal would lose interest and follow someone else. She had enough problems already. But instead, he lurched along at her heels. Even if she didn't look around, she could hear him breathing behind her.

They stopped for Ned's bike and, when they got to the Brainard house, slipped around the side yard to the back garden. It seemed a good idea to lock the dog in back and approach Mrs. Boehm carefully. However the housekeeper was in the garden picking parsley. Ned and Barbara didn't see her until it was too late.

She rose from a stoop to confront a gigantic brown and white animal that rushed toward her growling nastily. Dropping the parsley, she backed up until she was against the fence; there she stood, rigid with fear, not even able to scream.

Ned and Barbara ran after the dog shouting. Barbara flung her arms around it and dragged it to a stop.

"Down!" she shouted. "Stay! Stay!"

To Barbara's great surprise, the dog stopped, his sides heaving. He looked around to see what was holding him back, and left a wide smear of saliva on her sweater.

"It's okay, Tante Marg," said Ned confidently.

"Huh! Get it outa here," said Mrs. Boehm grimly. She stayed exactly where she was.

Ned picked up the scattered parsley and handed it to his aunt. "Well, you see, we—uh—we can't—that is—sort of. . . ."

"What you mean 'can't'?" She frowned until her brows nearly met; her jaw was rigid in her white face. "Get rid of that—that beast."

While Ned was trying, unsuccessfully, to placate Mrs. Boehm, Barbara ran to the garage and found a length of old rope. This she tied around the dog's neck; then she and Ned tugged until the St. Bernard allowed himself to be persuaded over to the fence post where the other end of the rope could be tied. Not until he was securely fastened, did Mrs. Boehm edge away from the back fence. She kept a wide distance between her and the dog, who lay down but growled whenever she looked his way. She went inside and banged the door.

"I dunno, Ned," said Barbara doubtfully. "Look how wild he acts. She won't put up with that, and my folks won't let me keep him even overnight if she threatens to quit."

"I'll talk to her," said Ned. "You convince the behemoth not to growl every time she looks at him."

"Do you suppose the way to a dog's heart is through his stomach?" said Barbara faintly. "Maybe I should feed him."

"Good idea." Ned swatted Barbara on the shoulder, drawing a deep growl from the dog. "I didn't mean it! I didn't mean it." He raised his hands in only partially mock terror and went after his aunt laughing. "Whether you like it or not, Brains, you have an admirer. And what an admirer!"

Barbara found Choto's empty dish and filled it with dog food from the container under the sink. Then she looked doubtfully from the dish to the St. Bernard. It didn't look as if that piddling amount would go very far toward filling him up. Sighing, she runmaged in the cupboard for the lower part of a dutch oven, filled it, poured in some milk, and took it to the post where the big animal lay.

He lay with his chin on his paws; when she set the dish down, he eyed it longingly but didn't move.

"What's the matter with you? That's good food," she cried in exasperation. He was being a lot of trouble, that was for sure. He looked at her, then at the dish, then at her again. "Go on—good dog. Eat," she commanded.

It was the magic phrase. He lowered his muzzle to the bowl and began to eat, almost inhaling the food like a vacuum cleaner. Barbara filled a second dish and then a third before he showed an inclination to slow down. Finally, he polished off the last crumb, gave a huge belch and began to pant. As Ned came out of the house, the dog gave a soft growl.

"And that's another thing," said Barbara severely, shaking her finger and stamping her foot. "You aren't to growl at us. It scares people. You'd better be good to us. You don't have many friends."

The dog rolled his eyes at her and went on panting. "You aren't to growl at Mrs. Boehm either," Barbara went on firmly. "You can't stay if she won't let you—you might not stay anyway," she added beneath her breath. Then looking at Ned, she said, "What did Mrs. Boehm say?"

He lifted his shoulders slightly. "She thinks we're nuts, but at least she hasn't given an ultimatum." Barbara stood up and tried to brush the dog hair off her pants. She looked as if she had been rolling in loose fur.

"Ned, this is insane. Look at him. He's gigantic. My folks won't let me keep him. He'll probably eat hundreds of pounds of food a day. And we've already got one dog."

"Yeah, but isn't he magnificent?"

They turned back to look at the dog. He lay sprawled along the fence, his heavy front paws stretched before him, panting and watching them.

"He's smart, too. He knows we're talking about him." As they watched, the feathery tail began to thump and he moved the heavy flaps that were his ears to show he was listening. Barbara couldn't help but think how gorgeous he was.

"Notice, he's stopped growling at me," said Ned. "He never did really growl at you."

"And, hungry as he was, he wouldn't eat until I told him it was okay. Someone's trained him."

"What'll you call him?" said Ned grinning.

"I'm—I'm not sure. I've been thinking. . . ." She paused and shrugged sheepishly. "I don't even know I can keep him—or if I want to."

"He knows," said Ned. "He's decided."

"Unfortunately, he doesn't have the final word," said Barbara opening the kitchen door. "Mrs. Boehm probably does."

"Why her? She's the housekeeper."

She shrugged. "Dad doesn't notice what's going on, and Mom doesn't care so long as the household runs smoothly."

"In that case, I'll put in a good word. Haven't I already?" He hooked his finger under his armpits and thrust out his chest, making Barbara laugh. "Tante Marge's a good sort."

"What if his owners turn up?"

"Well, of course, that'd be better," he said soberly. "But I hate the idea of any dog going to the pound, especially one as gorgeous as this one."

She agreed heartily.

They found Mrs. Boehm dubious but halfway resigned. Evidently Ned was a great favorite of hers. He did seem able to coax her into anything. He should be a diplomat, thought Barbara. Unfortunately, he wouldn't be around when her parents came home. But maybe the dog's owners would want him back. Maybe there'd be a big reward. She decided she'd divide it with Ned.

[twelve]

BARBARA WAITED for her parents on the bottom step of
the staircase. She sat with her chin in her hands,
Choto on her feet. Occasionally she scratched the limp,
silky ears.

"You tell me, Choto, will I get to keep him?
Should I keep him? How can I keep him?"

Choto pressed against her, saying nothing. She
hadn't even laid eyes on the St. Bernard as yet. Just
then headlights flashed across the front windows. A
car pulled in the drive and stopped; there was the
sound of a door, and then Barbara heard her mother's
steps across the porch. She walked slowly, so she must
be tired. The front door opened, Jessica stepped into
the hall and leaned against the wall, closing her eyes.

"What a day! I don't care if I never see the inside of an operating room again," she said. There was
the sound of a car going slowly around the house.

Barbara didn't comment. She'd heard that com-
plaint before. Tomorrow, after a night's rest, her

mother would head for the hospital as if it was the thing she most wanted to do.

"What're you doing here, Barb?" asked Jessica. "You look like you're waiting for Christmas."

"No—n-not that, but there is something I should. . . ." She got no further before the silence of the night was shattered by loud, angry barking and snarling.

"What the hell!" Jessica straightened up staring.

"Oh, no! Not that!" moaned Barbara. She shot off the step and dashed for the back yard. There was little moonlight, but enough to see two figures: a man standing rigid by the car, and the St. Bernard, still tied, lunging frantically toward him. How long the post would stand was in doubt. Barbara could see it swaying already. She jumped off the porch, as Jessica shouted, and ran toward the dog.

"No! I told you! Bad dog! Down, I said. Down!"

He heard her and instantly dropped to his belly, muzzle on his paws and peered up at her whimpering.

"I told you, no growling, didn't I? Bad dog." Speaking sternly, she shook a finger at him; even in the darkness, she could see his tail thump and his eyes roll.

"May I presume to ask what this is all about?" asked her father mildly. His voice seemed oddly calm considering. "It looks like the Hound of the Baskervilles—sounds like him, too."

"Well—uh—he probably isn't staying," said Barbara desperately.

"Staying!" said Jessica shrilly.

"I mean—uh. . . ." Barbara stood up and backed away slowly. The dog lay where he was, eyeing her reproachfully. "I think he thought he was guarding me. He didn't mean anything."

"If he didn't mean anything, I'd hate to have him really angry," said Jessica faintly as she held the back door open. "I've never seen such a gigantic dog in my life. It is a dog, isn't it? Where on earth did it come from? What's it doing tied to our fence?"

"Well, that's what I was going to tell you," said Barbara. "It's a little complicated."

"We'd like to hear about it," said Jessica wryly. Griffith left the car where it was, and they went inside. As her parents ate their late supper. Barbara explained about finding the dog, its hunger, Ned's coaxing her into bringing it home. She did tend to emphasize his coaxing a little bit.

Predictably, Jessica said at last, "What about Mrs. Boehm?" Dishes clattered noisily in the kitchen.

Barbara nodded faintly. "Ned talked to her. She hasn't said absolutely no. And I'm telling him—the dog—to behave. He—he's sort of trained."

"Trained!" snorted Jessica.

"Well, after all, just now he was probably awakened from a sound sleep. He did mind when I shouted at him."

"I'll say this," said Griffith mildly, "with a dog like that, you don't need to worry about protection."

"Yes, I can sure see that; but who's going to protect us from the protector?" Jessica took a deep breath. "All right. He can stay for tonight anyway—but how are you going to explain him to Measle and Choto?"

"I'll do it in the morning. They'll get along fine," said Barbara with a confidence she didn't feel. When the noise had started, Choto had leaped off her feet and disappeared. She was probably cowering upstairs; heaven only knew where the cat was.

Drat Ned anyway. If it hadn't been for him . . . on the other hand, she had the honesty to admit, it had really been her idea. All Ned did was point out that the dog seemed to like her; and she knew she wouldn't have been able to just walk away and leave him when she realized how starved he was. But what would she do about Measle and Choto? The little dog was so tiny, the St. Bernard might think she was a mouse. Did dogs that size chase mice? What if he stepped on her—or sat on her? And what about Measle? Sometimes cats didn't take kindly to an additional pet. He had accepted Choto, though. So maybe it would be okay.

"At least things are quiet now," said her father as he finished his coffee and stretched. "I hope it lasts. I'm dead tired." Shutting his eyes and leaning back, he rubbed his temples. It was what he always did aftre an especially long day.

Jessica put down her cup and went to massage his shoulders and the back of his neck. "Didn't the Carson surgery go okay?"

He nodded and shifted one shoulder so she could rub harder. "Oh yes, but it took a lot longer than I expected."

Barbara left them there in the dining room. For as long as she could remember, she had always thought of them like that, together. Even when separated, they always seemed to think alike. Maybe it was because they were in the same profession. She didn't know. In fact, she seldom gave it any thought. They went their ways; she went hers. Although lately, the relationship had been changing, getting closer.

Choto and Measle blinked sleepily in the sudden brightness as she snapped on the lamp beside her bed. Choto wagged her small body all over and tried to pretend she hadn't been sound asleep. The cat didn't care; he stretched his front legs as far out of the basket as possible, yawned widely, showing neat, sharp fangs and pale pink tongue. Barbara stooped to stroke them and ruffle Choto's ears.

"We have a new addition," she told them seriously. "I hope you get along. He needs a home—at least for a while."

The white, tie-back curtains shifted slightly as warm June air drifted through the window carrying faint fragrances of roses, newly cut grass and unidentifiable herbal smells. Barbara curled up in her maple rocker and leaned against the sill. It was dark outside, of course, but a bright moon cast a swath of silvery light across the back yard; it made the shadows an even blacker velvet and distorted familiar shapes.

She could see a rounded, dark lump beside the fence that was the St. Bernard. Even in the dark and curled in a heap, he looked big. But at least he was quiet, she thought, remembering her father's hope for a good night's sleep. Measle jumped into her lap and rubbed against her arm, purring steadily. It was hypnotic and suddenly she felt very sleepy. It had been a full day; tomorrow would take care of itself.

The moon shining down on the darkened house was dimmed suddenly as a cloud slid silently in front.

Against the fence, a dark shape lifted its head, sniffed the air and lowered it, blending with the other shadows.

A DOOR SLAMMED somewhere early in the morning, rousing Barbara. Remembering simultaneously about the dog in the garden and the day—Saturday—she hastily jerked on a T-shirt, jeans and sandals. It was vital that she be in the garden before Ramon arrived. Choto and Measle followed her downstairs but stopped in the kitchen hoping for breakfast. They would wait; Mrs. Boehm wasn't there yet, and Barbara had other things to attend.

The big dog was awake and watching the door. When she appeared, he struggled to his feet and strained against the rope, making the post lean dangerously. Barbara ran over, grabbed the rope and tried to pull him back down to the ground. She had no effect, except that he was so glad to see her; he pushed her flat and stood over her drooling and panting.

"Get off!" she cried pushing at him. It was like pushing a mountain, but eventually he did move his front feet, allowing her to scramble to her knees. His tail wagged slowly from side to side as he breathed moistly into her face.

"What am I going to do with you?" She sighed and bit her lip. He really was an awfully big animal.

For answer, the dog nudged his food dish until it hit the fence post with a thump.

"Okay. Okay. I understand." She untied the rope

and turned toward the kitchen, wondering if he would follow or run the other way and what she could do if he did. Or what she wanted to do if he did.

But he moved beside her, panting, toward the house. She climbed the steps without thought while he stood at the bottom and considered the problem. He was on the ground, but the person he had adopted was at the top; if he wanted to be with her, he had to go up the steps. Sighing, he struggled up to the porch and together, they entered the kitchen.

Barbara had forgotten she had left Choto and Measle there waiting for breakfast. As the door swung shut behind them, she saw the cat and the small dog the same instant they saw the St. Bernard. Choto began to tremble. The cat's fur stiffened, and his back arched until he looked three times his normal size as he hissed like a rapidly boiling kettle. The St. Bernard glanced around but didn't move from Barbara's side. To Measle, he still looked like approaching doom; the cat abandoned the floor and shot up toward the top of the highest cupboard. In his terror, he missed his footing and for a few agonizing seconds, his rear feet scrabbled wildly for a foothold. Finally, he pulled himself up on the shelf and retreated to the furthest corner where he huddled, peering over the edge, his eyes wide and black.

Thoughtlessly, Barbara laughed. The St. Bernard hadn't moved, hadn't even seemed aware of the cat, and Measle looked so funny. Choto, also, hadn't moved. Indeed, the little dog appeared to shrink as she peered at the huge animal. Her curly tail drooped for a moment and then wagged tentatively, hopefully. She was smaller than his head, but she wasn't retreating.

Barbara decided the best thing to do was to feed all of them. Perhaps eating together would help them get acquainted. She set Choto's dish on the floor about four feet from the dutch oven. The St. Bernard waited until Barbara gave him the command, "Good dog, eat," and then began to gobble the food without hesitation. Choto edged over and also began to eat, occasionally glancing up to see what the St. Bernard was doing. She must have felt reassured because she ate steadily.

With the two dogs busy, Barbara fixed the cat's breakfast, but coax as hard as she could, she couldn't get Measle to come down from his refuge. He crouched, frowning, just out of reach so she couldn't grab him even by standing on a stool.

"Okay, Measle," she said finally, "you can stay there." She put the cat's dish up on the cupboard and climbed down as Mrs. Boehm entered the kitchen.

The housekeeper stopped in the doorway and glared at the big dog, who ignored her; he was too busy eating.

"*A kutya!*, *Oriasi kutya!* What he doing in house?" she said pointing a shaking finger. Her English had become almost incomprehensible, but her expression and gesture were plain.

Barbara put her hand on the dog's shoulder. He glanced sideways but went on chewing steadily.

"I'll put him out as soon as he's finished," she said hastily. "But, see. He's not vicious. He was hungry last night. Choto's not scared." The little dog wagged her tail at the sound of her name.

"Humph." The housekeeper sniffed and edged her way to the dish cupboard, all the while keeping a suspicious eye on the St. Bernard.

"He better keep his distance," she said frowning. "Little dog one thing. She okay. He a *hegy*."

"We'll wait a few days," said Barbara coaxingly. "Maybe his owner will turn up."

"Maybe. Maybe not." She banged down the toaster slide. "He not stay in my kitchen. Kitchen only hold one dog, one cat, one cook."

"Of course. I know he's too big for the house. He can be in the yard."

Mrs. Boehm continued to frown; her lower lip pushed out like a small pink shelf and she snapped up the toast slide. The toast had begun to smoke.

"*A fene egye meg!* What if owner no claim him? What then?" she said accusingly. "You no try to keep him."

Barbara sighed. Here it was. Ultimatum time. She had hoped the housekeeper would be more flexible, maybe even come to accept him. As it was, things didn't look promising. If only there had been more time for Ned to work on her. There was silence in the kitchen for a moment, except for the burbling of the coffee and the dogs' steady munching.

Perhaps sensing that he was the subject of controversy, the St. Bernard looked up at Barbara and wagged his tail slightly.

She dropped to her knees beside him and put her arms as far around the heavy shoulders as she could.

He wagged again and went back to eating. Choto finished her bowl, looked at him, hesitated, and carefully put her nose into the dutch oven beside him. He ignored her intrusion, except to eat faster; together they finished the bowl.

"See!" said Barbara delighted. "He's not mean. Choto likes him."

"She likes his breakfast, you mean," said Mrs. Boehm firmly. "Better we find his owners."

"The problem is," said Barbara carefully, "if his owners don't turn up, what can we do with him?"

The housekeeper shrugged. Her knife sliced neatly through an orange, quartering it. She placed it on a plate and set it and a glass of milk at Barbara's place. "They have places—human societies."

"You mean humane societies. But there isn't one in Berea, Ned said. We only have the city pound."

"So?" Mrs. Boehm laid a warm cinnamon bear claw beside the orange.

Normally Barbara loved Mrs. Boehm's cinnamon bear claws. This morning she hardly glanced at it. "The pound can only keep a dog three days, then they des-destroy it." Her voice broke on the words, and she laid her head along side the furry neck. The dog in question looked up at Mrs. Boehm; his eyes drooped sadly. Even his jowls looked sad. "How could you even consider turning him over to the pound?"

"They not do that—not to handsome dog like that. He a-a monster—but handsome," said Mrs. Boehm grudgingly.

"I'm afraid Barbara is right," said Jessica. She

stood in the doorway yawning but dressed for work. "The pound can't keep unclaimed animals. They have no choice."

"Huh!" The housekeeper hated to acknowledge defeat. Instead, she filled a cup of coffee, quartered another orange and put it and a bear claw on a plate.

Jessica started toward the table, looked at the dog and stopped. "That's all well and good, Barbara, but I'm late and hungry. Will he take my arm off if I try to eat breakfast?"

"No, no. He'll do what I tell him. You'll see. He didn't growl at all at Mrs. Boehm, did he?"

She shrugged and pursed her lips.

Eagerly, Barbara began to rub the heavy coat and scratch the limp ears. "Now, you mustn't growl, mustn't be cross," she said. "We're your friends. Good dog. That's a good dog."

He rolled his eyes at her, wagged his tail and lay down, sighing, with a loud thump. After sniffing the huge feet cautiously, Choto lay down beside him. They both began to pant. Choto's small pink tongue barely showed below her jowls. The St. Bernard's thick red one hung down like a large section of underdone bologna. Even Mrs. Boehm had to smile.

"As soon as Ramon gets here, I'll take him out and introduce him," Barbara said. A great weight lifted for her. The first hurdle seemed to be successfully cleared.

The following days were busy. Between feeding the pets and practicing French, the time rushed past. Mrs. Boehm seemed reconciled to the presence of the big dog, at least for a few days, so long as he stayed in the yard. He even accepted the presence of Ramon without more than a token growl.

But Measle refused to adjust. He mostly stayed upstairs and never ventured into the back yard even to sun himself beside his favorite hydrangea bush. He was eating poorly, too. Barbara worried, but Ned said the cat would need time; that it would all work out.

He and Barbara and Margery discussed a name for the dog. He couldn't remain the Big Dog, or Him, or Hey You forever.

"What about Gargantua?" asked Margery. They were eating a snack on the back porch. The dogs were sprawled close together under the maple tree. Occasionally, Choto would reach over and wash her friend's large feet.

"Um. I dunno. Gargantua is awkward, and Gargy sounds funny."

"How about Paul Bunyan. He was big. Or Babe, his ox?" said Ned.

"Babe's too common and Bunyon sounds like something's wrong with his foot."

"Well, then, you think of something," said Margery dryly.

"How about a mountain? He's as big as one."

"They're not very furry," said Ned skeptically. "Do you know any cute mountains? Everest? Whitney? Shasta?"

"Well-ll."

"It's a problem," said Margery thinking hard. "Gollom wasn't lovable; neither was King Kong. Who was the giant in *The Tempest?* He was sort of lovable—at least he wanted to be loved, and I guess that fits this one." She nodded toward the dog.

"Caliban," said Barbara. She repeated the name over to herself. "I think I like it." She whistled. "Choto! Caliban! Come."

Immediately, Choto pricked her ears, leaped to her feet and scampered over to the humans on the porch, wriggling all the way. Barbara repeated the call. The big brown dog regarded her carefully for a moment then he lurched to his feet and shuffled over to the bottom step where he stood regarding them sadly.

"He likes it," cried Ned. "He knows his name."

So Caliban it was. No one claimed him, and soon it seemed that Caliban was a permanent resident of the back yard. He stopped growling at the family or friends, and Barbara's father began to buy dog food in hundred pound sacks. Only Mrs. Boehm and Measle withheld acceptance. Both of them kept their distance, but at least so far the housekeeper hadn't given notice. Still, Barbara lived with the worry that she might. And what about Measle?

[thirteen]

ONE MONDAY toward the middle of July, when Barbara went to lunch under the maple tree, only Margery sat there, munching a peach. She frowned and shook her head when asked about Ned's absence.

"Dunno. It must be serious. If he's absent twice more, he'll lose credit for the whole summer term."

"It was Emily," Ned explained the next day. "She had a bad attack, and I had to stay with her because Mom had to work." He looked tired and worried and ate Eloise's sandwich automatically without noticing, probably without tasting it.

"Did she forget her medication?" asked Margery.

He laughed without humor. "Not with everyone in the family remembering for her. She took it, and she still had a convulsion."

He began tearing little pieces of bread off and tossing them toward waiting pigeons. "Mom 'n Dad didn't find out till they got home from work Monday. They're pretty upset."

"I don't understand," said Barbara. "Emily's had seizures before, hasn't she?"

"Yeah," said Ned, "but we thought it was controlled. She hadn't had one since she began taking the phenobarb over a year ago. And now this." The brown paper lunch bag crackled in his clenching fingers.

Margery shook her head sympathetically. Barbara couldn't think of anything to say either. Emily was just a little kid—for that matter, Ned was a kid, too. They weren't supposed to face responsibilities like this. Life sure wasn't fair.

Lunch ended promptly, and the three friends went separate ways. Barbara resolved to tackle her father again about Emily. Surely there was something. . . .

But when she got home, her attention was diverted.

"I think Measle sick," said Mrs. Boehm, looking at the cat, who lay on his side under the table.

Barbara crouched down to look at him closely and stroked his fur. Choto came over to wash the cat's ears. Measle didn't move but lay stretched out, watching Barbara.

"He looks okay to me," she said finally.

The housekeeper shrugged. "Maybe. He no eat all day."

"He probably caught a mouse," Barbara ran her hand down Measle's side and felt his stomach as she had seen her father do. It did seem rather full. She resolved to watch him for a few days. Cats were funny —at least Measle was. Mostly he stayed close to home and ate well, but sometimes he'd be gone two or three days and wouldn't be hungry when he did return. She scratched his ears, was rewarded with a steady purring and got up to go do her homework.

"I'm sure he's okay," she said and forgot about it.

However, the next day the cat looked definitely ill; furthermore, he staggered unsteadily when he walked, and he refused the bit of roast beef Barbara offered him. Stricken, she cradled the cat in her arms and went to find her parents. Only her father was home.

"Dad, I think Measle's sick. He won't even eat roast beef."

Griffith peered over his glasses. "Maybe he just caught a mouse."

Barbara shook her head. "Mrs. Boehm says he hasn't eaten in days; he hasn't been outside either."

Her father lifted the cat onto his desk and gently palpatated the abdomen. Measle gave a soft cry of distress.

"You're right, I think, Barb. We'd better check it out." He handed her the cat and reached for the phone. "I'll give Frank Johnson a call and see if I can coax him into going into the office after hours."

She stroked the cat and tried to keep the tears out of her voice. She had ignored him in the excitement of Caliban's arrival. What if something happened now? She'd never forgive herself. How could she be so unfeeling?

Her father hung up the phone and reached for his sweater.

"Get me a towel to wrap the cat. Frank's going to meet me at his office."

"Can I come, too?"

He nodded. "You should. I can't drive and hold the cat, and you know how he hates cars."

Normally he hated vets, too, but this time he lay quietly and allowed the veterinarian to take his temperature, prod his middle carefully and look in his mouth with only a token whimper. Dr. Johnson nodded finally and began to fill out a card.

"He's got cystitis. Not uncommon, especially with neutered males, for some reason. He's feeling rotten now from autointoxication. We'll anesthetize him to remove the obstruction and keep him for a couple days to see how he does."

"How long will it be?" said Griffith.

Frank Johnson tilted his head and thought. "We'll see—we'll watch him for the next day or so. Telephone us on Wednesday."

And Barbara had to be content with that. She gave Measle a few gentle strokes and whispered, "You'll feel better tomorrow," before leaving with her father. But wasn't it lucky, she reflected on the way home, that her father was able to get such prompt care for the cat. What if her father was a bookkeeper or car salesman, then how would they have fared? Maybe it was good, sometimes, to be a doctor. This way, Measle would be better quickly and be home in a couple of days.

She continued to feel confident about Measle until Wednesday when she telephoned from school.

She went numb with shock when she heard the receptionist say, "He's not doing well at all. He came through the surgery to drain the bladder, but he isn't eating and he's getting weaker. I don't know what prognosis to give you."

"Thank you," Barbara whispered numbly. She hung up and walked stiffly back to Ned and Margery who were finished lunch and discussing part-time jobs and which was better, baby-sitting or paper-delivering.

"All the same," Margery was saying, "I'd hate to get up at dawn every day."

"It's better than—" Ned stopped as he noticed Barbara's frozen face. "What's wrong, Brains? Measle isn't . . . ?"

She sank to the ground gripping her hands together so hard the knuckles turned white. It was almost impossible to get the words past the fear in her throat. Swallowing, she said, "He—he's awfully sick. The receptionist said he won't eat, and he's getting weaker. The prog—prognosis is—is doubtful. And it's all my fault." At that she gave up trying not to cry and let the tears stream down her face.

"No, it isn't, Brains," said Margery gently. "Sometimes cats get that bladder problem. It's just one of those things." She patted Barbara's shoulder sympathetically.

Ned began to weave blades of grass together thoughtfully, not looking at her.

"I had a cat once," he said finally. "It hated hospitals and hated being away from home; it wouldn't eat either. Maybe that's what's wrong with Measle."

Barbara shook her head dolefully. "Even if it is, what can I do about it? He eats things for me, he won't for anyone else. If he were a person, I could visit him but. . . ." She stopped and stared hard at Ned. What if. . . . "Do you think I could visit him?" Ned and Margery gaped at her. "If he's so sick, maybe they'd let me see him. I bet he'd eat for me."

"I don't know," said Margery carefully. "I've never heard of such a thing."

"Why not?"

"Well—maybe. Isn't Dr. Johnson a sort of pal of your father's? I guess, what have you got to lose?"

"I sometimes help clean cages over there," said Ned. "I know Veronica, the receptionist. Want me to go with you?"

Barbara nodded, wiping her cheeks with the back of her hand. Already she felt immensely cheered; even if they couldn't change things, Margery and Ned were friends. They tried, and they cared.

"Come on, Brains, don't take all day," said Ned. "We can stop at Schaum's Market and pick up some liver. I bet he'll eat liver."

"That's his favorite."

It wasn't a long walk to the pet hospital, but they were both sweating when they arrived. Their bikes were at home, and Barbara didn't want to take the time to get them. The veterinarian wasn't in, but Veronica was and she approved of the reason for the visit.

"I think cats get sicker from loneliness here than for any other reason," she said. She even offered to cut the liver into small cat-bite-size pieces.

"Just a few," she said as she sliced. "I'll put the rest in the frig. Too much might cause diarrhea. We don't want to give him more problems than he has now."

Measle lay stretched listlessly in the back of his cage, staring out. His emerald eyes were dull, and his coat looked rough. His dish of cat food lay untouched beside him. But when he heard Barbara's voice, he struggled to his feet and staggered over to the small door. She put her hands in to stroke his head.

"Good kitty," she crooned. "Good Measle. I've brought some liver. See." She held out a piece of meat.

The cat sniffed it doubtfully, but as she continued to stroke his back and coax, he licked the bit of food and then began to chew. Ultimately, he ate several bits of liver before Veronica decided he'd had enough. When Barbara left, reluctantly, she had the satisfaction of hearing Measle purr; it was a faint, wobbly purr, but still a purr.

"I think he's over the worst now," said Veronica. "Now that he knows he isn't deserted. Call us tomorrow. Maybe you could see him again."

Barbara went to see him twice more, and each time, Measle looked more like himself. Then three days later, Griffith brought the cat home. Barbara still felt guilty; she knew her pets trusted her, and she felt she had let one of them down. Also, the problem of Measle and Caliban still existed. No one had come to claim the St. Bernard, and as the days passed, Barbara grew more and more attached to him. While she loved Measle, she also loved Choto and Caliban. But what if the cat never accepted the bigger dog. It had taken him a while to accept Choto, who was small. How could Barbara choose? And she might have to.

She sat at the window most of the night staring at the moonlight as it moved across the yard; while high in the sky the uncaring moon stared down. What could be done? The next morning, she was so heavy-eyed at breakfast, her mother asked whether she had slept.

Barbara propped her head against her hand, trying to remember if she had done her French homework. She shook her head at her mother. "I'm worried about Measle and Caliban. What if he won't accept him."

Sipping her coffee, Jessica nodded solemnly. "I know why you're concerned, but maybe it's unnecessary, Barb. Maybe part of the reason Measle carried on so was that he was getting sick. Why don't you wait and see—give everyone extra attention; but let Measle take his time. Cats don't like to be rushed. And I've usually found that what I've worried about most never happens."

Since Barbara had no better solution, she tried to follow her mother's advice. She even passed up a skating party with Florence and Mary Jane to walk the dogs, and she packed some catnip into Measle's favorite toy mouse. The cat was recovering and getting stronger, but he still showed no signs of wanting to go outside. Cats could be indoor animals, Barbara knew, but he had been an outdoor cat, and she often found him sitting at the kitchen window gazing longingly at his favorite spot under the hydrangea. Margery and Ned had no suggestions either.

There were other worries and problems, too. The *Plain Dealer* had reported a series of burglaries in the area; they were committed evidently by the same one or two men. The thieves tended to beat up victims who happened to discover them at work. Griffith changed locks on the doors and issued orders that even though it was hot the first floor was to be securely locked at night and whenever they went out.

It was inconvenient having to carry a key all the time, and Barbara complained about it to Margery and Ned at lunch. Neither of them sympathized with her much.

"My mom always locks the place like we owned the crown jewels," said Margery. "She forgot I was at a movie with Mary Jane and Florence one night and I didn't have my key. She went to bed early and she sleeps so soundly, she doesn't hear the doorbell. I had a terrible time getting in."

"I know," said Barbara. "And it's a good idea. I don't want the house broken into either, but still. . . ."

"How's Measle?" said Ned, changing the subject.

Barbara shrugged. "He's lots better, but he still won't go outside. He doesn't act afraid of Caliban any more, but he looks at him through the glass and frowns. If he doesn't exercise, he might get sick again."

Margery shook her head. "That dog. What a monster. I don't know but what I agree with Measle. I'd be afraid to go outside, too."

"And Mrs. Boehm doesn't like him either," said

Barbara soberly. "Poor Caliban. He can't help being so big." She knew what it felt like to be unwanted.

"Your folks must really care about you to let you keep him with all the trouble he is," said Ned.

Barbara had never given it much thought. "Um. Maybe. I dunno. They're always busy at the clinic. It was the same in San Diego. They don't pay much attention to home problems or to me."

"Brains, how can you say that?" protested Margery. Vigorously she began to stuff lunch things into the brown paper bag. "Your mom came to the play at school, and she talked to us a long time at your party. Lots of mothers never come to anything at school, and mine barely got home before we went to sleep at my slumber party. She had to work. I know that. And your mom works, too."

"She doesn't have to. Dad makes good money," said Barbara stubbornly.

"But she's a doctor. You can't just put it down and pick it up like—like a model train," said Ned. "With all the time and money it takes to become a doctor, you can't expect her to just drop it. And look at how your father took the cat to the vet as soon as he knew Measle was sick."

"And Mrs. Boehm doesn't like Caliban. He growls at almost everyone, but you've still got him," said Margery.

"Well-ll, I know, but. . . ." Barbara still felt there was something missing somewhere.

"Life isn't like a book—or TV program," said Ned soberly. "I have a great family, and we love each other, but with eight of us around, how much time do you suppose either Dad or Mom have for us individually? And the money's pretty tight, too. And sometimes we just plain get on each other's nerves."

"You always seem to be having such a good time," said Barbara.

"Sure, and we do. But you don't notice the other times—when I can't go somewhere because Emily's sick, or because it costs too much."

"Or that I've worn the same jeans until they're way too short," said Margery sticking out a leg to illustrate. However, since she was wearing shorts, this example failed, and they all giggled.

"I guess you're right—sort of," said Barbara after a while. "Maybe my folks do care. It's just that they're always so busy. . . . I guess the grass is always greener in other families' yards." She took a deep breath. "Okay. I'll try to understand my parents. Maybe they're trying to understand me." She scratched at a mosquito bite vigorously. "I must admit we've been getting along better the last few months."

"Good," said Margery, fanning herself. "And probably Measle and Caliban wil make friends, too."

"I sure hope so."

Ned looked up at the gray sky and held out his hand. "We'd better get home. I think it's gonna rain.

Margery sniffed the air. "It smells like it."

Barbara didn't understand how they could be so sure; however, the sky was covered by heavy, lowering clouds, and the air felt oppressive. She got to her feet with the others and started walking briskly toward home. They didn't make it, for the first large drops started falling before they reach Elm Street.

"Good night to stay home," said Margery as she turned down Cedar at a fast trot. Ned wasted no time in going his way.

Barbara agreed. It would be a good evening to make fudge or popcorn. She hoped her mother wouldn't be very late; her father wouldn't be in at all; he was out of town at a seminar. Then she thought of Caliban out in the rain. Maybe Mrs. Boehm could be coaxed into letting him spend the night in the kitchen. It was raining hard by the time she ran up the steps to the front porch.

The housekeeper was putting a casserole in the oven, and she nodded as she saw Barbara.

"*Jaj!* Barbara. Oven is set at 350°. I turn on now you home. You take out in thirty minutes, *nem*."

Barbara shook out her wet jacket. "Sure, but you aren't going out in this weather, are you?"

"Sure. Sister Olga invites me for dinner and movie maybe. Is okay with your mother."

"It's a rotten night to go out."

Mrs. Boehm shrugged. "Alla same. I used to rain." She smoothed her hair, put her apron in the closet and took out her raincoat. By the time she was ready, sister Olga was honking out in front. Mrs. Boehm hesitated about leaving Barbara alone.

"Dr. Brainard said she be home by six for sure," she said doubtfully.

"Go ahead. I'll be all right. It's after five now," said Barbara firmly.

As soon as the front door closed, Barbara was out

on the back porch calling to Caliban. Although he was huddling in the shelter of the garage, he was thoroughly wet. He blinked at her sadly as she stood on the porch.

"Good dog. Come, Caliban," she called again.

He responded as he always did, but it took time for him to get to his feet and move across the yard. Wagging his tail, he stood at the foot of the steps and peered through the rain at her. She went down, took hold of his collar and pulled to show what she meant.

"Come on, Caliban. I know you hate steps, but come on anyway. Good dog."

Laboriously, he struggled up the steps and into the kitchen, where he instantly shook vigorously. Water flew in all directions. Barbara was slightly quelled by the thought of what Mrs. Boehm would say when she saw the spots on her immaculate walls. Oh well, maybe she could wipe most of them off later. Caliban needed drying off, too. She found an old towel and rubbed the dog vigorously. He rolled on his side, stretched across the kitchen floor and sighed with pleasure. Choto came in to sniff his feet and sat down gingerly, away from his dampness.

Barbara laughed. He looked so comical lying there covering most of the floor. The front door slammed; the sound of high heels came clicking down the hall. Jessica entered the kitchen shaking her coat and shivering.

"Br-r! It's wet out there. What a night!" She dropped a kiss on the top of Barbara's head. "What's with the monster?"

Caliban rolled up on his elbows and flopped his tail.

"I brought him in because of the rain. He could catch pneumonia out there," said Barbara.

"Not likely through that fur coat. But he can stay, at least tonight. What's for supper?"

"Mrs. Boehm put a casserole in the oven; she just left a couple minutes ago." She looked at her mother, who was leafing through the mail and sorting it into piles; one to read and one to throw out. "When's Dad coming home?"

"Tomorrow night. He phoned this morning and told me what wonderful weather they're having. Ugh!" Jessica tossed out one stack of mail. "How about having dinner on trays in front of a fire?"

"Oh, great!" Barbara scrambled to find the TV trays. "But who—that is, can you fix a fire, Mom?"

Jessica laughed. "You bet. I used to go camping in college."

It was inconceivable to Barbara that her mother had ever been someone who went camping. Nevertheless, half an hour later, they were seated in front of a comfortably blazing fire eating the casserole. Jessica's shoes were off and she had changed to a blue corduroy housecoat that darkened her eyes and made her appear about five years older than her daughter. Barbara leaned back against the chair, listening to the rain beat on the windows and watching the flames flicker and snap. The warmth and peace were hypnotic. She felt about ready to drop off to sleep.

"I'm glad I brought Caliban inside," she said yawning.

Jessica yawned, too." He probably didn't even notice the rain." She yawned again. "Wow, I'm sleepy." She covered her mouth with long fingers. "Think I'll turn in early for a change. You're almost asleep, too. Mrs. Boehm'll be late, but no reason to wait up. She has a key."

Barbara agreed. She patted Caliban, who opened one eye, thumped his tail and went back to sleep. Upstairs, Choto and Measle shared the wicker basket. Everything was peaceful. Outside, the wind had stopped and the rain beat gently on the windows and made trickling sounds down the chimneys and gutters. It sounded as if it was letting up; maybe it would even be a fine day tomorrow.

It took only a moment for Barbara to fall asleep. She was roused hours later by a small sound. She listened and heard no more. The rain had stopped, it seemed. Then she heard a distant thud, and Caliban gave a loud growl.

Drat, she thought. Mrs. Boehm must have come in by the back door and wakened him. She'd be terrified—and angry as well. Barbara knew she ought to go down. On the other hand, it was so comfortable in bed. She waited for more sounds, but all was quiet. Mrs. Boehm must have ignored him. Good for her. Maybe she was secretly learning to tolerate him. On this happy thought, Barbara drifted back to sleep.

She was awakened in the morning by a piercing shriek, followed by an instantly recognizable growl. Groaning, she shot out of bed. Why hadn't she gotten up last night? Why had she assumed everything would be all right? If Caliban cornered Mrs. Boehm and wouldn't let her into her own kitchen—that would be the last straw as far as the housekeeper was concerned. Without stopping for robe or slippers, she dashed down the stairs and into the kitchen.

Mrs. Boehm was standing in the doorway of the dining room, both hands to her face, her eyes bulged with terror. She was staring across the kitchen at Caliban who lay in the corner by the closet, growling nastily. Behind him stood a man in rumpled, wet jeans who pressed himself stiffly against the closet door. Barbara couldn't see his face because he wore a black ski mask over his head, but she could see him trembling.

Behind her, Jessica gasped.

"My God! A burglar! Call the police!"

She was the one who finally made the call. Mrs. Boehm wouldn't, or couldn't, move. Every time she tried to enter the kitchen, Caliban lifted his muzzle, showing heavy front fangs, and growled. Barbara felt she might make him stop, but on the other hand, as long as he lay there, the burglar stayed where he was. The mask gave him an evil, inhuman look, devoid of all expression. How had he gotten in? What was he after? That was a stupid question, she thought. He was after money and stuff, of course. She thought of her allowance in the glass jar on her dresser. Would he have come into her room while she was asleep? She shivered. It didn't bear thinking about.

These questions turned out to be what the police wanted to know, too. At last they arrived, two men in blue uniforms, who looked like rescuing marines to the women—and it turned out, to the burglar, too.

"Oh, geez—thank God," he said when the men entered the kitchen. He stepped away from the closet door. Caliban lifted his head, drew back his lips and snarled.

"My God," said one of the officers. They stopped immediately.

The burgler pushed back against the wall. "Call 'im off, someone. Willya."

Barbara edged forward, forgetting her lack of robe or slippers. "Good dog," she said cautiously. "Good Caliban. It's okay, boy. Good dog."

He flopped his tail and rolled his eye sideways at her. She gained confidence. Taking his collar, she said firmly, "Let him go. Down, Caliban."

The dog resisted a moment; then he gathered his muscles, struggled to his feet and allowed Barbara to lead him down the hall.

The younger officer took off his hat to scratch his head.

"Well, well, will you look at that," he said.

"Geez, I'm glad to see you," said the burglar. The cop pulled off the mask, revealing a weak face with a vicious smile.

"Never mind. Up against the wall. I'm sure you know the routine," said the balding officer.

"If it isn't Jay Mertz. I thought you might be behind these break-ins. Where's your pal, Skinny?" said the young, blond officer.

Mertz shrugged. "I dunno what yer talkin about."

"Have it your way," said the officer. "Let's see what's in your pockets."

In short order, the items were laid on the kitchen table, including a short length of chain and a switchblade knife. The balding officer turned to the three women.

"How, ladies—and Miss," he said including Barbara. "How did you discover this—ah suspect?"

Jessica told her story. It was short, since she had slept soundly all night.

"I don't usually sleep that hard," she said, sounding aggrieved. "I must have been pretty tired. Anyway, I didn't hear a thing until Mrs. Boehm screamed this morning."

"Barbara didn't know much more. She had heard a thump and Caliban had growled sometime after the rain had stopped.

"That was around eleven forty-five," said the blond cop.

Mrs. Boehm was the star of the show. At first she found it difficult to speak; she stared at the chain and knife and kept swallowing.

"Take your time, ma'am," said the balding officer. "He can't go no place. He won't hurt you neither."

"I—I come 'bout twelve-fifteen," she whispered at last. "Sister Olga drive me. She wait till after rain. I come in kitchen, go to put away raincoat. He there—" she jerked her head in the direction of Caliban. "I scared. He growl. I real mad at you." She managed a weak smile for Barbara. "I can't put coat away. I go to bed."

"You didn't turn on a light?" said the younger cop.

She shook her head. "What for? I know kitchen. Was some light. Enough to see across to hall."

"I seen ya, lady," said Mertz sullenly. "I nearly said somethin'. That beast had me backed against a wall."

"Why didn't you?" said the older cop. "You must have been standing there all night.

"I sure was." He rubbed his back. "The house was all dark 'n quiet. I come in through the winder, see. Then that—that thing come at me. He woulda killed me. You got a vicious animal there, kid." He glared sullenly at Barbara.

"He is not," said Barbara indignantly. "He was just protecting us. You shouldn't have—" Her mother's hand on her shoulder stopped her; she could feel the hand trembling.

"Anyway, I got against a wall, and I been here ever since. The dog sat an' watched me fer a while an' 'en he lay down on my feet." He shifted as if they were numb and rubbed his face.

Mrs. Boehm's eyes bulged, remembering the dark kitchen of the night before. "You was there when I come home." She spoke faintly but accusingly.

He nodded.

"Why didn't you say something?" said the blond cop again.

"I figgered the damn dog'd go to sleep an' I'd get away—maybe even take somethin' fer my trouble."

Jessica shuddered and slipped her arm around Barbara. Now that the mask was off, Barbara thought he didn't look particularly evil, just sullen and rather stupid. However, the chain and knife were sober evidence of what he had intended.

"God, I'm tired," said Mertz rubbing his shoulders. "That damned dog went to sleep on my feet." He sounded put out. "He even snored."

"You could've gotten away then," said the bald cop. "It was stupid to stay and get caught."

Mertz shook his head. "Believe me, I tried. I just moved a toe 'n that damned dog woke up. I could've lost a leg. Ja hear 'im growl?"

His listeners agreed. Caliban had sounded serious when he threatened. A few minutes later, Mertz was led, handcuffed, to the patrol car, and the three men drove away. As they left, the balding cop turned to Barbara."

"You've got a valuable protector there, Miss. He deserves an extra nice breakfast. We've been after this guy and his friend for weeks. It won't take long to pick up the second man now."

Barbara agreed and evidently so did Mrs. Boehm. She stirred an extra large scoop of hamburger into his dog food.

"He good dog," she said setting the dog bowls in front of the stove. "I be hurt—maybe dead, if not for him." Her hands shook so that the bowls clattered against each other.

"I think he deserves a steak," said Jessica. Her voice was shaky, too. "When I think that with all that locking up, someone still broke in anyway—and what might have happened—I—I'm glad Caliban was here, that's all."

"Think what Dad's missing," said Barbara. As she spoke, she looked up to see Measle watching from the security of the top of the cupboard. He looked like the Cheshire cat, peering over the edge.

"Look!" she pointed. "He must have been here through all this."

"Too bad he can't testify," said Jessica shakily.

There was no way of knowing how long the cat had been there or why he had chosen this night to investigate the kitchen. When Barbara had gone to bed, the cat had been sharing the basket upstairs with Choto. He had to have known that the St. Bernard was indoors for the night; his nose would have told him that much. Whatever the truth, neither cat nor dog was revealing. Choto and Caliban were eating heartily, and when Barbara put the filled cat dish on top of the cabinet, Measle did the same. He seemed to have passed a crossroads.

When the dogs went outside, Barbara was surprised to see the cat follow, keeping a cautious distance and showing no interest in them at all. A few days later, there was another cold snap, and Barbara found both Choto and Measle curled up against Caliban's broad side. Trust a cat to know where it was warm. But warm or cool, she felt suddenly lighthearted. Maybe the almost burglary hadn't been such a bad thing after all; at least, good came out of it, since both Mrs. Boehm and Measle had begun to accept Caliban.

Measle still pretended distain or fear, but Barbara noticed he spent more and more time lying close to the big dog. If Caliban was in the back yard,

Measle would be under the hydrangea bush; at night —for Caliban now spent his nights snoring happily in the kitchen—the cat slept either with Choto in the basket upstairs or in the kitchen against Caliban's furry back. Mrs. Boehm would sneak treats to both dogs; and she told everyone who would listen how Caliban had saved her life, and she didn't even know about it until the next morning.

"Jaj! Such a good dog it is." She invariably ended with a pat for his broad head.

Jessica threw up her hands in mock dismay.

"What a zoo," she said. For it now looked as if Caliban had permanently joined the household; certainly there was no doubt but that all of the human members slept better at night because of his presence.

[fourteen]

CALIBAN SEEMED to be a contented family member, appreciative of a filling meal every day and an occasional scratching behind the ears. He preferred the out-of-doors, which was just as well. He had a tendency to knock over small tables or sweep the contents of the coffee table onto the floor with one wag of his tail. When something crashed, he always looked around with an air of puzzlement that Barbara found exasperating. He would wag his tail whenever she was around, and if she scolded him, he looked penitent but he still wagged his tail and he still knocked over small objects. Measle would sit on the couch, his toes tucked in, and look superior, as if he were thinking, I told you so.

If the doorbell rang while the dogs were in the house, Caliban rushed down the hall barking joyfully and threw himself against the front door. To make things worse, Choto joined him, adding her high-pitched yap to the confusion and getting generally underfoot. So everyone agreed that the yard was the place for the dogs except at night. Before retiring, Mrs. Boehm always set out a bowl of water, and before she took Choto upstairs, Barbara coaxed Caliban up the back steps and into the kitchen, where he spent the night snoring happily against the back door.

A steady diet filled out his hollow spaces, and he gained a considerable amount of weight. Gradually he stopped growling automatically at everyone; however, Barbara remained the only person who could scold or punish him. When she did, he would cower in a corner and whimper sadly.

"Probably you remind him of someone who cared for him and whom he trusted," said her father grinning wryly as he watched her try unsuccessfully to push past a two-hundred pound block of fur. Caliban was the greatest user of passive resistance Barbara had ever seen; the dog simply lay down and what could anyone do about it. He was at the same time both a source of pride and a tremendous problem.

As the summer passed, she discovered she had less time for reading and even less for pretending to be someone else. She found it difficult to imagine an appropriate literary parallel when she was soaking wet as a result of bathing Caliban and Ramon was laughing because she looked so funny. Even Jo March never had to contend with a St. Bernard. It would have been great to stroll casually down the street, dressed in the latest fashion, with him on a fancy leash. But he soon scuttled that plan.

She took him out once, but he snarled and lunged at the first person who approached her. The man wasn't bitten, but both he and Barbara were frightened, and she admitted Caliban should be left in the yard. His protective instincts were too great. Choto learned to walk on a leash, but she didn't have the same dramatic appearance as a St. Bernard.

Barbara's birthday was the end of July and, for the first time in her life, she wanted a party.

"A dinner party, please," she coaxed, "but not a whole lot of people."

"On behalf of Mrs. Boehm, we thank you," said Jessica.

"Just the Ferris kids and the sixth grade group from Room 100. That's not many."

"It's fifteen, not counting you," said her mother doubtfully.

The housekeeper smiled broadly and shrugged. "I no care. Parties fun. I fix big cake, eh?"

"Oh, thank you. Thank you." Impulsively, Barbara hugged her. Mrs. Boehm looked embarrassed and awkwardly flapped at her shoulder with a potholder.

Invitations went out, and everyone accepted. Looking at the list, Jessica asked about all Ned's brothers and sisters. Was Barbara going to expect a present from everyone?

"I dunno, I guess. I really didn't think about it," she said. "We've just talked about games and such."

"But you've said before that they don't have much money. That's eight presents from one family. Even if Ned earns money, he's saving for college."

"Gosh, I never thought." She felt badly about that. "But what can I do? I didn't mean it like that. I

was just thinking of having a party and having fun."
She often thought that money, its presence or absence,
sure caused a lot of trouble.

Her mother tilted her head in consideration.
"Well, it's too late to say it's no birthday party. We
could say no presents requested at all. Would it bother
you not to have anything to open?"

Barbara hesitated and shook her head. "I guess
not. Not as much as worrying about whether they
could afford it. Besides, you and Dad'll give me something, won't you?"

Laughing, Jessica stood up. "I think you can rely
on that." She looked at her watch. "I've got hospital
rounds to make in half an hour. Why don't you ask
Mrs. Boehm. She'll understand, and she'll be back
from market soon."

Barbara hemmed and hawed, not quite sure how
to present an idea, that while it was meant gener-
ously, might be taken as an insult. She needn't have
worried. When the housekeeper sorted out the various
I mean's or you know's, and understood Barbara's intention, she chuckled and shook her head.

"Here," she said handing Barbara some cereal
boxes. "Put on top shelf. You got young legs." She was
still chuckling. "You good girl, Barbara. Mean good.
But no need. Kids like parties. Like give presents.
They make things. You see. All kids happy about
party. I fix great cake."

She bustled about the kitchen chattering happily
while she put away the groceries.

Barbara left her there and went to find Measle,
although Choto or Caliban would do, for company.

Now she could look forward to her birthday. What would her parents give her? She'd been too busy with other things to think of asking for anything special. But Dad almost always came through with something unusual. Last year's birthday, her main present had been an overnight cruise on the square-rigger ship in San Diego bay. So what would this birthday bring?

The week before the twenty-sixth had never dragged quite so slowly before. Barbara did her homework, groomed Caliban and Choto, cleaned her room and still had time to nag Mrs. Boehm about the menu and to offer to taste things until the housekeeper took her by the shoulders and firmly pushed her out the door.

"Go play," she ordered, "brush dogs, read. But stay out of kitchen. Cake no good if worried over."

Barbara sniffed. She didn't feel like doing any of those things. Her homework was finished and all her friends were busy. It was Saturday, so Ned would be collecting and Margery had a baby-sitting job. Maybe she'd take Choto for a walk. She was hunting for the leash when the phone rang. It was Ned.

"Hi, Brains. Say, can you do me a favor?" he asked.

"Sure—at least maybe," she said cautiously.

"It's really for Emily. The other kids are going to the zoo with Tante Olga. Emily said she'd rather come see you and Choto. She's probably too little to walk through the zoo anyway. I'd stay home, but I have to collect. So—if it's not too much trouble, can she visit you this afternoon?"

"Of course. I'd love to have her. I'm not going anyplace anyway."

"You're sure?" He sounded so relieved, she was glad she had been free. "I'll bring her over on my bike."

Barbara ran to tell Mrs. Boehm. "Emily's coming over this afternoon. I'll be baby-sitting."

The housekeeper frowned. "For why? You no baby-sit."

She drew herself up with dignity. "Just because I never have doesn't mean I can't. Besides Ned asked me. The others are going to the zoo, and Emily doesn't want to go. She asked to come here."

"Ah, I see." The housekeeper sighed and went back to stacking the dishwasher. "Okey-doke. I here anyway."

Would Ned have brought Emily over if his aunt were somewhere else? Barbara wondered. Feeling somewhat deflated, she went outside to sit in the swing. Why was Margery mature enough to take care of children and she wasn't? Ned could hold two jobs, but she couldn't. Was she going to be kept in cellophane forever?

Gripping the ropes, she leaned back, stretched out her toes and began to pull herself through the air. Gradually, she swung higher and higher. The smooth back and forth was soothing; the breeze rustled through the leaves and gently brushed her cheeks. If she leaned way back, her braids dragged on the ground on the downswing and she could point her toes to the sky. She hadn't done any swinging all summer; there hadn't been time. Now it made her feel better.

"Brains! I want to swing!" called a voice. Emily stood on the driveway with Ned just behind her.

"You were miles away," he said grinning as she dragged her feet on the ground until the swing slowed enough so she could jump off without breaking a leg.

"I haven't done that in a long time—not since just after we moved in," she said. "Come on, Em. I'll give you a push." She helped the little girl onto the seat. "Hold the ropes tight or you'll fall off."

She began to push Emily with gentle, steady strokes. Ned watched for a moment smiling and then, with a wave, he left.

"Bye," he called. "It'll only be for a couple hours."

"Higher! Higher!" Emily shouted delightedly.

Barbara pushed until she was winded and her arms ached.

"You'll have to stop, Em. I'm exhausted," she said finally, sitting down on the porch panting.

"Can I swing tomorrow at your party?" Obediently, Emily slipped off the swing and sat down beside Barbara. Choto came over and squeezed in between them so both girls could pet her.

"Well, I don't know. There'll be a lot of people, and we'll be playing games and stuff." Seeing Emily's disappointed face, she added hastily, "But maybe you can, if there's time."

The little girl nodded. "I love to swing, and we don't have a tree in our yard."

"You could have one of those pipe frame things."

"We used to, but now there's no room. Papa grows vegetables instead."

"Oh, I'm sorry."

"Anyway, they don't go high enough," Emily said philosophically. "Next year, when I'm in school, I'll swing on the big ones and go way over the school yard fence."

Barbara smiled at her assurance. "But for now, since I'm tired, what do you want to do?"

"Read me a story."

"Okay. How about. . . ." She had to stop to think what books she had that Emily would like. "*Winnie-the-Pooh?* Have you read him?" Emily shook her head. "No? I'll be right back."

She ran upstairs to the back of her closet where her old books were stored. As she sorted through the box of books, she remembered the Raggedy Ann in the bottom dresser drawer. She found the book and the doll. Both showed a lot of use, but they were in good shape. Raggedy Ann's apron was wrinkled, but it was clean, and her smile was as steady as ever and her eyes were bright. Barbara held her a moment, remembering times when Raggedy Ann was her greatest comfort. She smoothed the smiling face. Raggedy needed to be loved. It wasn't right to leave her in a drawer forever. There came a time to leave dolls behind. She sighed wistfully; sometimes growing up was painful. However. . . .

She carried the doll and the book down to Emily, who had moved over to Caliban and was sitting on the ground petting both dogs. Barbara wondered about the allergy, but so far Emily was not wheezing.

"She was my favorite doll, Em. I'd like you to have her," said Barbara firmly, laying the doll in Emily's lap. "That is, if you want her."

"Oh, yes. Yes." Eyes bright, Emily picked up the doll and cradled her gently. "I've never had a Raggedy doll before. She's nice. Can I call her Raggedy Brains?"

"Of course. After all, she's yours now," said Barbara laughing as she picked up the book. She felt a twinge of regret, but Emily hugged the doll closely. She would take good care of her, and Raggedy Ann deserved a better fate than lying in a dark drawer.

Winnie-the-Pooh was a book Barbara always enjoyed reading, and Emily was an attentive audience. She sighed when Barbara finished.

"I wish it weren't over," she said.

"Why?"

"It's so funny. I like Eeyore." She grinned, crinkling her eyes at the corners.

Barbara looked at her watch. "It's getting late, but maybe I've got time to hunt for another one. Do you want a second story?"

"Oh, please," said Emily fervently. She moved to the swing, carrying Raggedy Ann/Brains. "I'll swing while you're gone."

"Okay, but be careful. Don't swing high," said Barbara. It would only take a moment to find the second Pooh book. She knew right where it was. But it took longer than that. She finally emerged, dusty and sneezing, with the book. On her way through the kitchen. Mrs. Boehm stopped her.

"You and Emily do okay?"

"Sure. Between the swing and reading Pooh, we're getting along great." She took two cookies from the cookie jar. "Is this all there is to baby-sitting?"

Mrs. Boehm shrugged eloquently. "Already you expert," she said. "Dinner at six. Your parents might be here. Might not."

Barbara sighed and nodded. "I know. Dad said he was so tired this morning, he wanted to be home early, take a hot shower and go to bed. Hope he makes it."

"No matter. Dinner a casserole."

"I hope he's here for my birthday."

"Sure. Tomorrow Sunday. They be here," said Mrs. Boehm positively.

"Maybe." Barbara was more realistic. She took two more cookies and went toward the back door.

Through the kitchen window she could see Emily. The little girl was stronger than she looked. She was swinging quite high; her short, pale red hair stood out from her head like a halo, and the skirt she wore in honor of the visit to Barbara's fluttered in her face on the upswing. Barbara grinned at how tightly she was clutching the stuffed doll.

"Don't try to hold the doll, too, Emily," she called from the back porch. "You might lose hold of the rope."

"I won't. See how high I can go!" Emily leaned backward as she had seen Barbara do. As she did, her movement made the doll slip from where she had tucked it and swing free, held only by Emily's hand on the rope.

It wasn't a heavy doll, but perhaps her hands

were sweaty. As Barbara hurried toward her in sudden fear, Emily's hands slipped.

Barbara called frantically, "Don't Emily! Let the doll fall. Hang on!"

But it was too late. Emily made a grab for the doll, lost her hold when the swing was at its highest point, and plummeted to the ground. She screamed just once as she fell. Then she lay quite still, the stuffed doll beneath her.

Barbara screamed just once, too, and ran to the limp little body. Emily's eyes were closed, and one arm looked strangely twisted. She didn't seem to be breathing either. Mrs. Boehm came puffing down the porch steps.

"Emily, what happened? You fall? You okay?" she cried. Her round face looked gaunt with worry and she reached out to pick her up.

"Wait," said Barbara sharply. "We shouldn't move her. It might make it worse."

"Not move her? That crazy!" said Mrs. Boehm. "No can leave here. Ground damp. And dogs!" Caliban and Choto had come over to see what happened and they were trying to lick Emily's face. Mrs. Boehm kept pushing at the St. Bernard, unsuccessfully trying to keep him away.

"Caliban! Choto! Come!" Desperation made Barbara's voice sterner than the dogs had ever heard. They looked at her in surprise, but they obeyed. She took hold of Caliban's collar.

"I'll call the clinic and get an ambulance or my father. You stay with Emily."

She didn't wait for an argument; Mrs. Boehm

always dithered and reverted to Hungarian when she was upset. She could get the dogs in the house and make the phone call quicker by herself. The operator answered on the second ring, but when Barbara asked for Dr. Brainard, she was told that he was in conference and couldn't be disturbed.

"This is his daughter," said Barbara using the same tone she had used on the dogs. "There is an emergency. I must talk to him."

It worked, and then her father was on the line saying calmly, "What's wrong, Barb? What's up?"

"It's Emily, Dad." Relief made Barbara almost gibber like Mrs. Boehm. He'd fix everything, she knew he would. "She fell out of my swing. She's on the ground unconscious or—or—" She couldn't continue.

"Don't move her," he said sharply. "I'll send an ambulance."

"Can't you come?"

"I'll see her here. Put a blanket over her. That's all." He hung up abruptly, but she hardly noticed. Her knees felt weak and shaky, but at least help was on the way. The afghan would do to cover Emily. Dad would know what to do. How terrific to have a doctor for a father. She remembered to lock the dogs in the kitchen. Caliban would never allow strangers with a stretcher even into the yard, let alone touching Emily.

Mrs. Boehm was sitting on the ground beside the unconscious girl. Gently, Barbara covered Emily and sat down on her other side.

"Dad's sending an ambulance. It won't be long."

The housekeeper nodded dully. "Can—can you tell if she—she's breathing?"

"I—I not sure. Not know how. . . ." Mrs. Boehm wet her lips and gently stroked Emily's hand. She was so white, and her eyes looked sunken. The vein in her temple showed blue through the skin. Barbara throught she saw a faint movement at the throat, but she wasn't certain. Emily wouldn't . . . she couldn't. . . .

The sound of a siren cut through her formless dread. Her father must have given directions because the ambulance didn't pause at the curb but, instead, swung up the drive, past the house and into the back yard. Within a minute or two, Emily was examined, carefully moved onto the stretcher and into the ambulance. Barbara and Mrs. Boehm watched numbly as the men pulled away. Neither of them had even thought to ask to go along. Emily had looked so small —just a slight bulge under the gray blanket.

Mrs. Boehm was the first to move. She struggled awkwardly to her feet.

"I got to—to go tell Sister Elsa. She don't know."

"Take me to the hospital first," said Barbara, jumping up. "I'll wait for you and Mrs. Ferris there." The housekeeper hesitated. "Besides, I—I want my mother." Desperately, she needed Jessica's calmness and assurance.

"You don't need to come, Barbara," Mrs. Boehm spoke awkwardly. She had to speak slowly or it came out in Hungarian. Untying her apron, she trotted toward the kitchen.

"Yes, I do. I couldn't stand it here at home." Barbara ran ahead, took the stairs two at a time, and hurtled through the kitchen. She barely glanced at the cake ingredients spread along the worktable. The big mixing bowl was partly filled with a pile of sifted flour that looked like soft snow. It was waiting for the eggs and such to be added with Mrs. Boehm's special touch. It would wait awhile longer; Barbara barely gave it a thought as she rushed past.

A book, that's what she wanted. She wanted a book to take to Emily. Maybe a fairy tale would be good. She found one, grabbed it and ran back down the stairs. On the way to the car, she saw Raggedy Ann lying on the ground where she had fallen. Picking up the doll, she scrambled into the front seat as Mrs. Boehm pressed the starter.

They didn't speak further. Barbara couldn't think of anything to say, and Mrs. Boehm looked as if she needed to concentrate on driving. She nearly ran a red light as it was.

The housekeeper stopped in front of the hospital; Barbara got out and remembered that Mrs. Boehm wouldn't know where to go.

"I'll be in—ah—I guess probably—I'll be in the emergency waiting room," she said. "It's around to the back. There's a big sign and you can't miss it. You'll be there as soon as you can?"

"Perhaps we wait at Sister Elsa's," said Mrs. Boehm. Her chin quivered so she could hardly speak. "I afraid of hospitals. People d—no good there."

"You must come," said Barbara firmly. She spoke as sternly as she had to the dogs. Mrs. Boehm's eyes focused suddenly, and her chin stopped quivering.

"They'll need permission to treat Emily. Get her parents here as soon as you can."

Blessing the earlier time spent in the hospital that gave her that knowledge, Barbara slammed the door before Mrs. Boehm could argue. She heard the car move away as she ran up the drive to the emergency entrance. How long it would take Mrs. Boehm to find Emily's parents and explain things, Barbara didn't know, but maybe she could help somehow. At least she knew a little of how things were done in the emergency room. And it was infinitely better than sitting at home watching a silent telephone.

Luckily Mrs. Evans was the nurse on duty. She was filling out some forms and greeted Barbara cheerfully.

"Well, hello, Barbara. Come to help us out again? We can sure use the time. Your father's down here. . . ."

"No—that is—I—I don't—" She gave up trying to answer the question, wet her lips and started again. "Where's Emily Ferris?"

"Who? Oh, the little girl who just came in? She's in Number Two. I'm just going to call her parents. . . . Hey . . . you can't go in there. . . ."

She spoke to empty air as Barbara walked rapidly down the corridor. Room 2 was the largest of the emergency rooms. She remembered it well. It looked just the same; someone in a white coat bent over the body of a small girl—Emily—and listened to his stethoscope. It was the resident. Where was her father? Barbara started to ask when Griffith came striding down the hall, his white coat flapping. He didn't look vague at all, but he was frowning .

"Barbara, what are you doing here?" he said brusquely.

"I—I thought maybe there was something I could do—give blood or—or something. . . ." She faltered.

"Just keep out of the way. Where are her parents?"

"They're coming. Mrs. Boehm's gone to get them. How—how's Emily? Is she—okay?"

"Don't know," he said briefly. "Have to wait for the X-rays and CT scan." He turned to the resident. "Where are they? Do they have to take all day?"

"They're coming STAT, sir."

No one paid any attention to her. Barbara pressed against the wall and watched numbly as figures in white moved around her. Someone brought a sheaf of X-rays. Her father slipped them into the viewer, snapped on the light and stared at them.

"Hmm. Doesn't look like a fracture—concussion?" he murmured mostly to himself. "But there's something here. . . ." He reached for the phone. "Page Dr. Schaumberg to emergency, STAT, please."

Barbara couldn't stand it any more. She slipped out of the room and walked aimlessly down the hall in the general direction of her mother's office. She needed Jessica more than she ever had. Her mother was using the dictaphone when she opened the door. She turned with an irritated jerk of her head.

"I can't be disturbed, Sara. You—why, Barb! What's wrong?" She put down the microphone and held out her hands.

227

Barbara threw herself in the chair beside the desk and blurted out the story of the afternoon and its consequences. She ended by crying. "And she's hurt—maybe—maybe—and it's all my fault!" She rocked back and forth in the chair hugging herself tightly and biting the inside of her cheeks until she could taste blood.

"Nonsense. This isn't the time for hysteria," said Jessica briskly. "You said Griff is with Emily now?"

Barbara nodded. "He—he just put in a page for Dr. Schaumberg. Does that mean Emily is—"

"Just that she might need surgery." Jessica put her arm around Barbara. "He'd want to have a second opinion. But Tom isn't in the hospital. He told me he was going camping. It isn't his weekend to be on call."

"But Dad won't operate on children," Barbara wailed.

"Of course he will, if he needs to. Let's go see if the Ferrises are here."

"I told Mrs. Boehm I'd be in the emergency waiting room," said Barbara meekly.

"A very good suggestion," said Jessica. "We'll go there as well. Maybe they're here by now. Maybe Grif can tell us some news."

Quickly Jessica dropped the dictaphone into its case. "Don't look so wretched, Barb. We don't know yet how badly she might be hurt. And it doesn't sound as if it was your fault either."

"No, but. . . ."

"I'll just tell Sara where I'll be." She stuck her head around the doorway to the small office next door, said something, and shut the door. "Okay. Let's go."

Having her mother beside her was a big help. Barbara's legs didn't feel so rubbery as she returned to the emergency rooms. Her father looked around as they entered.

"Hullo, Jess. Know where Tom is? I guess you heard about Emily Ferris," he said.

"Yes, Barbara just told me. But Tom's gone camping; I think he said Lake Milton."

"Damn! I forgot. He did say something about it on Monday." He clapped his hand on his head and stared at the exhibited X-ray.

"How is she? Any sign of fracture?" Jessica stepped up to the X-ray and studied it, too. "I don't see any."

"No. I don't think so. Just a concussion. But there's this dark area." He pointed to a fuzzy place on the film. "Isn't the little girl an epileptic?"

Jessica nodded and sighed. "She takes medication regularly. I suppose the shock of the fall might bring on a seizure. In any case you'll need to find out what she's been taking."

"Of course. But that's not the whole picture." He studied the X-ray a moment without speaking. "Who's her doctor? I'd like to check with him."

"I'll ask Mrs. Ferris. She might be here by now."

"Emily doesn't have a doctor, Dad." Barbara spoke timidly, through stiff lips. "Ned told me they just continued with the same medicine from before they moved here."

He frowned at her. "How did they get the prescription filled?"

"I don't know."

"Griff, what do you think it is?" Jessica briefly touched the X-ray with a long index finger.

"Well, I'd rather check with Tom, but it seems to me it might well be a neoplasm. You can see the location—the edges here—and look at the scan." He held out the long paper.

"Well, you know it's not my field," she said glancing at the strange diagrams. "But I'd go along. Will you operate tonight—if the parents give permission?"

He sighed heavily. "Probably. With the concussion, too, there's no point in waiting.

Standing against the wall, ignored, Barbara watched as her parents discussed procedure. Her father was reluctant to operate, but he seemed to feel strongly that it was advisable. While neurosurgery wasn't her mother's field, she at least knew the right questions to ask.

Finally, Jessica laid her hand on Griffith's arm and said soberly, "I don't see why you keep saying you want Tom. You're better than he is—for this sort of thing. You've even written a paper on it."

"I know, but I haven't worked on a child in a year."

"That turned out well."

Griffith bit his lip and studied the X-ray and scan. Barbara opened her mouth to add her plea when Jessica glanced at her and shook her head slightly. It would be her father's decision, she guessed, and probably it was better that way. It was a problem she was glad she didn't have. At last he sighed and snapped off the light.

"Okay, Jess. Let's go talk to Emily's parents. Where are they?

"Mrs. Boehm was to bring them to the emergency waiting room."

They walked together down the hall with Barbara trailing along in the rear, feeling very useless. The Ferrises were in the waiting room with Mrs. Boehm. They formed a tense trio that seemed oblivious of the ebb and flow of people around them. Ned was also there, but he stood beside the admitting desk, hands in his pockets, shoulders hunched, watching the nurses and aides working. He brightened when he saw Barbara.

"Hi, Brains," he said, jerking his shoulder nervously.

"Hi." She felt at a complete loss for words. He had trusted her, and as usual, she had loused it up. She couldn't find the words to express her feelings of regret and responsibility

He ran a hand through his hair and nodded at Barbara's parents. They were talking to Mrs. Boehm and Ned's parents. Mrs. Boehm waved her hands vigorously, evidently explaining something. Myron Ferris frowned and turned to Griffith. He had to look up to the taller man, but what Griffith said must have reassured him because he nodded and took his wife gently by the arm; he put his other arm around her as he talked.

"Gee, I'm glad you brought your parents," said Ned. "Maybe you can tell me what's going on."

Barbara shook her head slowly, "I don't know

any more than you do. I listened but it didn't do any good."

"How's Emily? Are your parents going to operate on her?"

"Mom won't. She's a thoracic surgeon. Dad might. He wants someone named Dr. Schaumberg, but he's out of town."

"Why should he want someone else? I bet he's better." Ned spoke firmly, his eyes admiring Griffith.

"That's what Mom says. I don't think Emily has a fractured skull. Dad said something about concussion."

"Oh. I suppose that's what they're talking about now." Both Barbara and Ned looked toward the small group. They were certainly talking, but occasionally one of the Ferrises seemed to ask something.

"Wish I knew what was going on," said Ned wistfully. "You're lucky to have doctors for parents."

"It doesn't help. I don't understand what they're talking about anyway." She hesitated, took a deep breath and touched his sleeve diffidently. "Ned, I'm sorry. It's all my fault."

"What is? You mean what happened to Emily?" He seemed truly surprised. "Don't be ridiculous, Brains. You didn't push her out of the swing. It could have happened when anyone, or even all of us, were around. Why Eloise fell off the porch and broke her leg when Mama, Tante Marg and Tante Olga were right there." He smiled a little crookedly at the thought. "In fact, she wasn't quite five—the same age Emily is now."

Barbara felt a great deal better, still upset, but better.

"You made that up."

"No, I didn't. Scouts' honor." He held up a hand, grinning sheepishly. "Well, maybe a little. She did fall off the porch, only she just sprained an ankle. She was bruised a lot, though."

"I see. Thanks, Ned." She turned away to look out the window. The long afternoon was almost over; soft gray shadows softened the outlines of the buildings and motorists had begun to turn on their headlights.

"It—it's almost time for dinner." The entire day was gone, and she hadn't noticed.

Ned didn't seem to have noticed either. They stood side by side looking through the window at nothing. Movement reflected in the glass caught her eye and she turned.

Her father strode out of the room and her mother motioned to her.

"Griff is going to operate," she said, speaking quickly. "Not for the concussion. It's a tumor, he thinks! Mrs. Boehm'll take you both home. I've got some work to finish, and then I'll be back to keep Emily's parents company.

"We want to stay, too, Mom." She was sure she could speak for Ned as well as herself. Partway along the corridor she saw two orderlies pull a gurney out of the emergency room, turn it smoothly and push it rapidly toward the elevators. Emily's small body made scarcely a bump in the smoothness of the sheet.

233

Barbara caught her breath and blinked back the sharp pain behind her eyes.

"You can't help," said Jessica, "and it'll be a long time."

"It doesn't matter, Dr. Brainard," said Ned. "Tante Olga is with the other kids. I've got to stay here."

"Mrs. Boehm can fix you supper."

"Please, Mom. I couldn't eat anyway."

"Or me, either."

"Well, all right. There is the coffee shop." Briefly Jessica laid a hand on their shoulders and walked quickly back down the hall.

For the group left behind, the hardest part, the waiting, began. Barbara began to empathize with those other people she remembered who stood or sat awkwardly on chairs that were always uncomfortable. People seemed to go to one of two extremes: they either talked constantly, frantically, or they didn't speak at all. The Ferrises were silent. They sat quietly, without moving, staring at the floor.

True to her promise, Jessica returned within an hour. She came striding down the hall, her white coat flaring out behind her, followed by two nurses with clipboards. At the waiting room entrance she stopped, wrote on the clipboards, said something to the nurses and came into the room.

"Come on up to the fourth floor," she said. "There's a waiting room right outside surgery; it's smaller and more comfortable."

"Will it be much longer?" ventured Mrs. Boehm timidly, once they were all in the elevator.

Jessica shook her head soberly. "I can't tell you. It's apt to be. Even once it's over, she'll be in intensive care awhile."

No one spoke during the rest of the ride to the fourth floor. As Jessica said, the waiting room was smaller and better furnished; also, they were the only people there. Downstairs, the doors swung constantly; people, both staff and public, moved in and out. Emily's parents and Mrs. Boehm seemed unaware of the confusion, but Barbara had been and she was grateful for the quiet. Not only that, the chairs were a lot more comfortable.

"I've sent for sandwiches," said Jessica. "There's a coffee urn in the corner."

"Thank you. I couldn't," said Elsa Ferris faintly.

"Must eat. Keep up strength," said Mrs. Boehm. She poured coffee for everyone but Barbara and Ned.

Time inched along. From the higher floor, they could look out and watch darkness spread across the city. As the sky blackened, streetlights sparkled like strewn diamonds on velvet. Only Ned and Barbara went near the windows, however. The others sat huddled together on the brown and beige striped couch. In spite of Elsa Ferris's original reluctance, when the sandwiches arrived, they soon disappeared. The aide who brought the tray even remembered glasses of milk for Ned and Barbara.

Food tasted better than she had expected and evidently Ned thought so, too; he quickly ate three sandwiches.

"Jeez, I've never known time to go so slow," he muttered as he and Barbara stared out the window.

"What are they doing in there?" He wagged his head toward the heavy double doors marked Operating Rooms Staff Only.

Barbara shook her head. "Wish I knew. I've never had any experience like this, but I've heard both Mom 'n Dad talk about how long some surgery takes." She hugged herself and shivered. "It's awful just waiting and feeling helpless. I hate being helpless."

"Me, too. But when I'm grown up, I won't be," said Ned grimly.

"How are you two doing?" said Jessica just behind them. She looked over their shoulders at the city lights. "It's beautiful at night isn't it? Everything looks so peaceful." A giant ruby of a light began to flash in the near distance and a siren split the air. "Except now and again," she amended soberly. She moved over to the coffee urn and poured herself another cup.

Barbara couldn't decide whether to admire her mother's control or be annoyed at her for not showing feeling. The hospital became quiet; visiting hours ended; and one by one the lights in patients rooms snapped off. Would the time never end?

"Ah—Brains, happy birthday," said Ned with a near smile. "This is a rotten way to spend it, though."

She looked at the clock over the door. "I guess it is —my birthday, I mean. I'd forgotten."

The steady slap-slap of footsteps sounded; without speaking, Jessica set down her cup and walked swiftly down the hall. She and Griffith met in the middle and stood talking for an instant. He still wore

236

the operating room greens, and even from that distance, Barbara could see his shoulders sag with fa-
tigue. Together they came down the hall to face the
waiting group. Elsa Ferris reached for her husband's
hand, and he put his arm around her. Mrs. Boehm
took her other hand, and Ned moved to stand with
them. No one seemed to breathe. But, as they came
closer, Barbara could see that they were smiling.

"Emily's fine. She stood the surgery very well. It
was a neoplasm—a nonmalignant tumor. We got it
all."

"Thank God!" said Mrs. Ferris and began to cry,
so did Mrs. Boehm; Mr. Ferris blinked very fast, and
Barbara clenched her hands and bit the inside of her
cheek severely. Ned shoved his hands in his pockets
and turned to look out the window.

"When can we see her?" asked Mr. Ferris.

Griffith managed a tired grin. "Not for several
hours yet. She's in intensive care, and she's unconscious anyway. Why don't you all go home and get
some sleep? Come back tomorow."

Jessica patted the other women on the shoulders.
"That's good advice. You're all tired out, and morning is time enough to see Emily."

"Can I see her, too?" asked Ned awkwardly.

"There's a closed-circuit TV here." She gestured
to the blank set in the corner. "It's only on during
visiting hours. You can see her and she can see you—
in fact all your brothers and sisters can visit her here."

"Emily is really all right?" Elsa Ferris sounded
as if she couldn't believe it.

"She's fine. She's a very healthy little girl." Griffith looked at his watch. "I need to get back. See you tomorrow." And, with a quick wave, he walked back down the hall.

"I take you all home now, yes?" said Mrs. Boehm.

"That's a good idea," said Jessica. She turned to Barbara. "I haven't forgotten your birthday, Barb. We'll celebrate it yet."

"I forgot it. It's not so important now."

"How about the party? Is it still on?" asked Ned.

Barbara stared at him blankly. "What party? Oh —gee—I dunno." She turned to her mother. "I forgot about the party, too. Should I have it or not?"

"How do you feel about it?"

"Well. . . ." It was difficult to tell. At two o'clock in the morning, how could anyone decide about a party? She was tired, and she knew everyone else there was, too. Mrs. Boehm hadn't finished the cake either. And, of course, Emily couldn't come. Maybe the other Ferris kids wouldn't feel up to it. She could just as well put it off for a week or two. The world wouldn't stop just because her party was late.

On the other hand, the other kids were looking forward to it. Mrs. Boehm had said so, and so had Margery and Florence earlier in the week. Maybe they would have just a sort of get-together.

"Could we just have the kids and maybe ice cream and hot dogs? Not anything fancy. It's a shame to disappoint everyone."

"You're right," said Jessica. "We'll keep it simple."

"I still make cake," said Mrs. Boehm positively. "Can bake in morning."

"Margarethe, you are to sleep late," said Jessica firmly. "Don't even set the alarm." It was the first time Barbara had heard her use the housekeeper's given name.

"I won't, Dr. Jessica. Thank you," said Mrs. Boehm meekly. "But I still make cake."

"Well, nothing involved, mind." Jessica nodded and grinned a little. Evidently the relationship between her mother and the housekeeper had reached a more casual state.

"That'll be great. I'll tell the others," said Ned as he stifled a yawn. "Suddenly I'm dead on my feet."

"Let's go home," said his father. "We'll see Emily tomorrow. Will you thank your husband, Dr. Brainard?" She nodded. "And thank you, too, for your concern as well."

Mrs. Boehm began to shepherd her relatives out the door; she looked at Barbara. "You coming?"

Barbara shook her head. "I think I'll wait for Mom. Thanks."

"Okey-doke. See you later. Happy birthday." She took her sister's arm and headed for the door. Mr. Ferris walked slowly after them.

Before he followed, Ned turned to Barbara. "I haven't thanked you for being here, Brains," he said awkwardly.

"That's okay. I didn't do anything."

"Just being here was a help. It made the time go faster—at least not so slow."

239

"Well. . . ." She flopped her hand sideways. There didn't seem to be anything to say. The greatest tension was over, but there would still be a long convalescent time for Emily and a great deal of patience was going to be needed by every one of the Ferrises. "See you at the party?"

"Right!" he said and managed a smile.

They left quickly after that, obviously glad to put the hospital behind them.

Jessica sighed and rubbed her temples. "God! It's been a long day. Aren't you tired?"

"Sure. But I'd rather wait."

It was the first time she had ever been in her mother's office, except for the few seconds earlier in the day. It was a small, cluttered room with one wall full of books and journals. There was a loveseat with a folded blanket and pillow; Barbara curled up immediately and Jessica spread the blanket over her.

"I've got a couple patients to check on, but I'll be back as soon as I can. Get some sleep," she said.

Barbara yawned widely and settled down. She was asleep before the door closed. She was awakened when Jessica shook her shoulder.

"Sorry, Barb, but it's time to go home."

"Oh—wow!" She yawned and stretched. "Boy was I asleep! What time is it?"

"Four a.m. and I'm beat."

Barbara struggled to her feet and tried to make some sense—at least to make her feet and legs work. She felt woolly-headed, as if she were wading through heavy surf, and it really wasn't worth the effort. To-

240

gether she and Jessica walked to the back entrance. The car was the only one in the corner of the physicians' parking lot.

"Are you the only one who works all night?" asked Barbara.

Jessica yawned. "No, of course not. It's just as it happens." She got in the car, hunted vaguely for her keys, found them and started the engine. Barbara rested her head on the back of the seat and looked at Jessica's profile. Her mother looked tired and disheveled; little wisps of hair made a halo in the flickering light from passing streetlights.

"Mom, what made you decide to be a doctor?"

"Why?" Jessica's face went blank at the sudden question.

"I mean, did you always intend to be one."

"No. When I was your age, I wanted to be a dress designer." They stopped for a red light and she smiled at the memory.

"You did? What changed you?"

She grinned broadly. "Someone told me I'd have to learn to sew."

"And now you stitch people."

"Well, that's not all of it," said Jessica wryly.

"No, I know. But. . . ."

"It's hard to say what made up my mind," she said slowly as she drove forward. "I always liked school, especially science. Chemistry and biology were my favorite subjects. Med school seemed to be a logical choice. But I didn't decide on the surgery bit until I was nearly through." She sighed and rubbed the back of her neck. "I think maybe I like the challenge of figuring out what's wrong with a person and then being able to fix it. I hate being helpless."

"That's what Ned and I felt last night. We hated it." Barbara locked her hands around her knee. "I suppose Dad feels the same way."

"He said something like that once." Jessica grinned. "We're alike in a lot of ways."

"Why did you marry Dad?" As her mother looked faintly shocked, she hastened to qualify her question. "I mean—well—did you date any other guys?"

"When I had time, sure." Jessica shrugged slightly. "I wasn't much interested in dating in high school, or college. In med school the ratio of men to women is about ten to one."

"Wow!"

"But that's no reason to go. Everyone has to study so hard, there isn't much time—or interest either—in social life. I was on a scholarship, too."

"I didn't know that," said Barbara thinking of Margery.

"Grandma and Grandpa didn't have the money to pay my way. Without a scholarship, I couldn't have graduated."

"Oh." No wonder her mother admired Margery's ambition. "Somehow, I just thought—that is, it seemed —I don't know," she wound up lamely. "I always thought of you as already graduated."

Jessica laughed gently. "No reason why you should. I don't dwell on it much myself. I'm just glad"

—she leaned, reached over and patted Barbara's knee—
"that you won't have the struggle I did."

"I can see that now, Mom," said Barbara soberly,
"but, you know, maybe sometimes, the struggle isn't
so bad." She thought back to the fun she had had helping Ned with the grocery carts and the closeness of the
Ferris family. Even Margery knew where she was
going and how she planned to get there.

Her mother stared at her soberly. "You're quite
right, Brains," she said at last. It was the first time she
had ever used Barbara's nickname. Barbara didn't
even know she knew it. "I don't regret the work I did
or the way I had to study. It's made me a better doctor. And I have more in common with my husband,
too. Maybe we've sheltered you too much."

Dawn was just beginning to turn the sky to pearl;
to the east, there was the suggestion of pink and gold
on the clouds. Jessica stopped the car in the drive.
They were home.

"I think I'll sleep late," she said stretching.

Barbara stared at the quiet house. She had never
been awake so late before; it was, she decided, yawning, a highly overrated privilege.

In the kitchen, the nightlight burned steadily.
Caliban lifted his head and thumped his tail; otherwise, the house was asleep. Barbara intended to soon
be likewise.

"Is Dad home?" she asked.

"I expect so. He signed out before I did." Jessica
sighed. "I'm for bed. It's been a long day."

"Me, too." Barbara pulled herself up the balus-
trade and was asleep within minutes.

It was almost noon when she woke and smelled fresh baking. Brilliant sunshine streamed in the open window; outside the sky was bright blue with only a few puffy white clouds floating on the horizon. Barbara leaned on the sill and sighed with contentment. The worry and tension of yesterday was past. It was a gorgeous day, and it was her birthday.

"Good morning! Good morning! Good morning!" Mrs. Boehm positively caroled as Barbara entered the kitchen. "Which you want? Breakfast? Lunch?" She took the cake tins out of the oven and quickly turned them on wire racks. They looked like dark brown, woolly saucers and smelled delicious.

"How about a little of both?" Barbara pinched off a crumb of warm cake.

"Get away! Not frosted yet. You jinx it." The houskeeper flopped a potholder at her. "Sit down. I make your favorite sandwich. Happy birthday."

"Thanks. Have you heard how Emily is? I suppose Mom 'n Dad are at work."

"Emily fine. She wake up, go back to sleep. Sister Elsa phone little while ago. Dr. Griff at clinic. Dr. Jessica in study." She poured orange juice and assembled a bacon, lettuce and tomato sandwich as she talked.

The food tasted great. She hadn't realized how starved she was; but then she had slept through breakfast and last night's dinner had been definitely sketchy. She finished eating and wandered into the study to see her mother, thinking about the housekeeper's new titles for her parents. Evidently they had taken on a new relationship, a less formal one. Would her friendship with Ned be any different now? No reason why it should really, but things didn't always work out the way one expected.

Look at Emily. All these years everyone thought her epilepsy could not be helped, and obviously it could. Would Mr. and Mrs. Ferris be happy about that or would they resent the years of worry?

Her mother was writing out checks in the study.

"Mom, I'm never going to get married—never!" said Barbara.

"What brought that on? She put down her pen and leaned back in the swivel chair.

"Being married is the pits," Barbara flounced into an easy chair and tucked a foot under her. "And having children is worse."

"I didn't know you felt that way."

"Well, I do. Look at all the trouble being married causes."

"Oh, I don't know. It's pretty nice a lot of the time."

"Maybe. But look at Ferrises. Mrs. Ferris has to work, and even so, with eight kids, they never have any money for anything."

"Money isn't everything, Barb," said her mother soberly. "The Ferris children have a lot of love and family life."

"And what about Mrs. Boehm?" She rushed on as if her mother hadn't spoken. "She planned a family life, and her husband died. Now she has to spend her time taking care of us."

"There aren't any guarantees, you know, of happiness or success. I'm sure none of the Ferrises wanted Emily to be handicapped, but they coped."

"That's another thing." Her voice rose shrilly. "Why did that have to happen. Why did she have a tumor? It isn't fair!"

"I don't know." Jessica twisted slowly on the swivel as she tried to sort her thoughts. "Life often isn't fair. When I was your age, my dog was hit by a car and killed. My parents told me the dog was in the hospital. I didn't find out for months, and I never forgave them for lying. It wasn't fair that my dog was killed, and it wasn't fair that my parents lied. Maybe it wasn't fair of me to not forgive them. But it happened."

"Oh, Mom," said Barbara sharing the long-ago pain.

"Now I know they did the best they could," her mother went on, "but I didn't think so then."

She rocked awhile in silence while Barbara thought of a young girl who lost her dog. "Sometimes," said Jessica, "I think we can learn from tragedy. Seeing Emily's acceptance and her family's patience and devotion can teach us to be more patient with our own problems."

"I suppose. I don't think I'm very good at accepting things."

"No," Jessica grinned. "I don't think you are either. But then neither are Griff or I. That's why we're doctors, I suppose."

"I'm tired of feeling guilty, too."

"Guilty? About what?"

"Oh, lots of things," she said vaguely. "You can,

you know, if you put your mind to it. First I felt guilty about all the trouble I kept getting into in school, but that didn't seem to help me any; then I brought Caliban home, and no one wanted him. Measle didn't like him, and then he got sick. It seemed as if it was my fault. And I was so proud when Ned trusted me enough to take care of Emily, but she fell off the swing and got hurt. That was my fault. And Dad wouldn't have operated if I hadn't called him. I know he won't work on children if he can avoid it. So if something had gone wrong, it would have been my fault again.

"That's quite a load of guilt," said Jessica soberly. "Ask your father when he comes home how he feels about it. But remember you can't take the blame for everything that goes wrong in the world. If that were possible, you'd have to take credit for what goes well, too, and that would be real arrogance."

"I never thought about it that way," said Barbara slowly. She sighed. "This summer has sure given me new perspectives."

Jessica smiled. "That's all part of growing up. You are, you know."

Yes, she supposed she was, Barbara thought. But even so, she'd ask her father how he felt about operating on Emily as soon as he got home. In the meantime, there was her party to get ready for. There really wasn't much to do, as it turned out. Mrs. Boehm preferred to cook alone and Ramon had left the yard in good shape before he went home on Saturday. So she brushed the dogs, who squirmed and wriggled with pleasure, gave her room a quick cleaning and set paper plates and things on the buffet in preparation for the picnic supper.

Before she knew it, it was four-thirty and her father arrived. He carried a stack of gift-wrapped boxes. She had wondered where her presents were hidden, but ever since she was seven and had found her Christmas gifts early, she had been careful not to look. There was too much of a letdown.

"Can I open them now, or do I have to wait?" she asked hopefully.

He tugged one of her braids and laughed. "Might as well open them now. It's been your birthday for quite a while."

Jessica laughed, too. "Go ahead, while it's quiet."

"How's Emily?" She began to shake the first box. It was small and fairly heavy.

"Doing fine. Her mother's been there all afternoon. Her father brought the kids for a few minutes. She has Raggedy Ann propped so she can see it, and she keeps asking the nurses to read Pooh to her."

Barbara sighed. "I'm so glad. She'll miss the party, but maybe we can have a coming out of the hospital party." She opened the box. It was a miniature telephone and a note. From now on she'd have her own phone. "Oh, thank you. That's just perfect. Now I can talk to Margery as long as I want." Telephoning hadn't been a real problem up to now, but it would be nice to phone in the privacy of her room. Her parents didn't listen; it was just the idea. The other boxes were clothes; a cashmere sweater set and matching wool pants, and a gift certificate to choose a bathing suit from Halle's.

"Maybe I can go shopping tomorrow," she said looking at the certificate. "There's over a month before school. I can get a lot of swimming in, now that summer school is over." She sighed extravagantly. "Only a month of vacation."

Jessica laughed. "That much less time to be bored." She turned to Griffith. "Barbara wants to ask you something."

"I do?—Oh, yeah." It took a few seconds to remember. "I was telling Mom how I feel guilty about a lot of things, like maybe Measle got sick because I brought Caliban home. And if the operation hadn't gone well with Emily, I'd have felt it was my fault. First because she fell on my swing and then because you probably wouldn't have operated if I hadn't called you."

Her father shook his head and stretched his legs in front of the chair. Barbara thought how different he looked in a sports shirt and slacks from the gaunt figure in the rumpled cotton green outfit of last night. He looked better this way.

"I appreciate your concern, Barb, but you overdo it. I'm a big kid now and old enough to make my own decisions. Surgery like that is never done casually; another opinion is always good. Tom would have called me if he'd been here. Since he wasn't, I would have been called whether you did or not. It was good, though, that you got hold of me directly. It saved valuable time."

"And I doubt that Measle holds anything against you," said Jessica pointing out the window. Caliban lay stretched full-length, his head on his paws, in the

249

deepest shade of the maple tree. Tight against his head was Choto; a few feet away, in a patch of dappled shade, pretending the dogs were invisible, was Measle.

Barbara chuckled with her parents. "He can sure be funny, now that he's decided Caliban is acceptable. I think he likes their company."

"So you see," said Jessica briskly, "your guilt feelings are unnecessary. Guilt is all very well. It's like a conscience and keeps us from doing reprehensible things; but it can be habit-forming. Don't feel guilt for being alive."

"Just do the best you can, that's all we ask," said Griffith.

"You don't mind if I don't even want to be a doctor?"

He shook his head. "Not if you'd rather be something else. We sort of took it for granted, because with both parents M.D.'s, getting into med school would be a lot easier."

"What would you rather be, Barb?" said Jessica curiously.

"I don't know." Events of yesterday had been confusing and unsettling; she found some of her previous convictions had been shaken loose. "I thought I wanted to write or maybe study languages. But sitting around yesterday, not able to help Emily was . . . was . . . a bummer," she finished lamely. "I'd rather be doing something."

"Well, fortunately, you don't have to decide this minute." Jessica began to gather discarded tissue paper and ribbon. "I think it's almost time for your birthday party."

Sure enough, the doorbell rang. It was Edward and Florence; Margery arrived soon after. They hadn't heard about Emily's accident, and by the time Barbara had told them all about it, the rest of the Ferris children arrived.

Byron reported that Emily looked pretty funny with the big white turban, but she waved to them on the TV monitor; and Ned said the Pooh book was her favorite.

"I'll send *The Wizard of Oz* tomorrow with Dad," promised Barbara happily.

The birthday supper was a big success. They ate on the back porch and slipped crumbs to the dogs. Mrs. Boehm outdid herself with the cake; even Jessica ate a large piece and Griffith and the boys each had two. Barbara felt she had never had a birthday so full of warmth and good wishes. Soon after dark, Ned announced that it was time to go; Byron and Edgar needed to get to bed. Edward, Florence and Margery made plans to go swimming after Barbara got her new suit; then they, too, left.

Barbara helped Mrs. Boehm and Jessica clear up. It didn't take long.

"I'm turning in early," said Jessica, "to make up for last night."

"Me, too," said Griffith. "I'll check the garage and bring in Caliban. Be right back."

"Tired, too," said the housekeeper. "But happy." She looked as if she was nearly asleep already.

"Me, too. Thank you everyone for a super birthday," said Barbara fervently.

With Choto beside her, she climbed the stairs, already thinking about the bathing suit she would choose and the swimming party on Tuesday. She lay quietly in bed, savoring the good feeling, listening to the buzz of crickets and watching the moonlight creep across the floor. What a change twenty-four hours can make, she thought. Yesterday was awful, and today was great. It was marvelous to be twelve.

[fifteen]

On Monday Barbara found her bathing suit almost immediately; she was in luck because end-of-summer sales were on, so she could get a matching terry beach robe, too. Mrs. Boehm's eyebrows rose, and she shook her head as Barbara modeled it delightedly.

"You three-fourths naked."

"Everyone's wearing these. It's not nearly as skimpy as some."

"I know. Even so. . . ." She frowned and sighed. "Why wear anything?"

Barbara chose to ignore these mutterings. She liked the outfit; it was her favorite color combination, scarlet and pale blue. Of course, she felt a little self-conscious at the way her figure was emphasized, but no doubt she'd get over that. After all, she would soon be in junior high.

Even though she was early at the pool on Tuesday, Edward, Mary Jane and Florence were ahead of her. They had worn their suits so they didn't need to use the dressing rooms. Barbara admired their fore-sight as she tried to keep her clothes off the soggy cement. By the end of summer, the building smelled of mold, age and sweat.

"Don't worry," said Florence when she com-plained. "The pool is closed for three months—Novem-ber, December and January. They give it a good air-ing and sometimes repainting. It'll smell better when it opens in February for swimming classes."

"Phooey. Who wants to swim in the winter?"

"Hardly anybody. That's why it stays in good shape until July," said Mary Jane lazily. She lay stretched on the grass, her head pillowed on her bent arm. "Am I even?" She turned over to sun her front and then sat up with a squeal.

Dwight was hanging on the pool, giggling and flicking water on her.

"You—you child!" she said indignantly.

Dwight assumed an injured expression. "You were all so busy, I wanted your attention. I wanted to ask Brains how Ned's sister's doing? What's the gory scoop on the surgery?"

Barbara had to laugh; she flicked a towel at him and made him duck. "How did you hear?"

"Oh—somewhere. My sister ran into Eloise, I think."

"Well, Emily's doing fine. She had a tumor."

"And she'll be okay?" said Edward. "That's great."

"I'm glad," said Florence simply. "Emily's a good kid."

"Can she have visitors?" said Dwight.

"The operation was only Saturday. I don't think anyone but her parents can see her yet."

"Why not?" said Dwight. "I don't like hospitals myself. Don't ever intend to go to one. But what about her brothers and sisters?"

Edward shook his head. "They don't let you visit in hospitals or clinics unless you're over sixteen."

"That's dumb," said Dwight. "Kids ought to be able to see other kids."

"They worry about infection and colds and such," said Florence.

Dwight shook his head in disgust, but Barbara decided she'd rather talk about something else. "Anyway they have a closed-circuit TV there. Ned and the other kids can see her on it and she can see them. Has anyone seen Margery? I phoned but there was no answer so I suppose she's baby-sitting somewhere."

"At her sister's," said Florence making a wry face. "She didn't want to, but her mother insisted."

"She baby-sits all the time. I thought she had a job lined up for August," said Barbara.

"She did, but her sister needs her and she doesn't pay very much."

"What a shame," said Barbara, her voice muffled under her arm. The sun felt warm on her back and the grass tickled her bare back. "It's too nice a day to work."

"Yeah, but think of the money," said Dwight. "Ned's working, too, probably. He must be, or he'd be here."

"He told me he's already saved enough for his freshman year in college—and he's not even officially in high school; that's what I call looking ahead," said Edward sounding envious.

"Sure—but it's still too bad to have to work on holidays, even," said Barbara.

"It's the breaks," said Mary Jane philosophically. "If you can't get to college except on your own. This is my last summer to loaf. I'll be working next summer. But I'm lucky. Dad's going to pay me to help in the store."

"Would he give me a job?" asked Dwight. "Think how much fun it would be to work in a delicatessen."

"He couldn't afford it," said Edward, laughing. "You'd eat up all the profits."

"Only until I got sick to my stomach," said Dwight. He dipped his towel in the pool and wrung it out on Edward's back; Edward leaped up and pushed Dwight into the water. As he fell, he grabbed Edward, who fell in, too.

"C'mon, I'll race you three times around the pool," shouted Dwight after he coughed the water out of his throat. The girls joined in, and no more was said about Emily or hospitals or work.

A WEEK BEFORE school started, Emily came home, walking slowly with the aid of a chromium walker. She moved slowly and still needed to spend most of the day in bed, but she looked well and laughed a lot. The turban was gone, and her head was covered with soft, curly red fuzz. All the children vied for ways to help or favors to do until Ned said it would be a miracle if she didn't turn into a spoiled brat.

"Be glad she's home and well," said Margery laughing. "Emily'll be all right."

Nevertheless, when Emily asked for an extra dish of ice cream and pouted when there wasn't any, her mother told her firmly to mind her manners.

"She's still recovering," said Barbara softly to Ned.

He shrugged. "She shouldn't feel sorry for herself. We all have to take turns and she's no different from the rest of us."

"But she's been through so much."

"Who hasn't? A lot of people are worse off than she is—or we are. A lot of people are better off. That's the way of the world. We can't afford self-pity. That's a waste of time."

The next day the sixth graders (now seventh graders) from Room 100 met and talked about senior high.

"What I'm worried about," said Barbara, "is having only a dinky locker to keep my stuff in. I expect I'll forget the combination, too."

"I know I will," said Margery, nodding.

"I suppose it's too late to flunk and stay in Room 100," said Florence, wistfully.

"That's silly." Edward sighed with resignation. "You know if we flunked, we'd be transferred to a different room anyway."

"Well, maybe it won't be as bad as we've heard," said Mary Jane.

"It can't be as bad as we're imagining," said Ned. "Things seldom are."

Autumn was creeping across the land; there was

a mild nip in the air at night, and there seemed to be a franticness to everything the group did, as if they would never have another summer vacation.

Even Barbara was caught up in the tension. She tried at the same time to extend summer vacation and get ready for junior high school. She swam in the public pool, exercised the dogs and tried, unsuccessfully, to coil her hair like her mother's. She sorted her books and her clothes, and then organized a tag football game in the park.

But, inevitably, the day came. Barbara woke with a feeling of anticipation. She leaned out the open window trying to assess the weather and decide what to wear. Instead, she saw Ramon and remembered the first day she had seen him. She had thought he was marvelous; he had such intense brown eyes and a terrific smile. But he wasn't interested in anything she was interested in. He only wanted to talk about his car or his job. Of course, he was going to marry Margery's sister anyway. But she found it didn't matter; he was only a pleasant young man who did the gardening.

In the distance, the bells rang out from the campanile on the university campus. Time she was getting dressed; there was a lot to do before school. She'd wear a short-sleeved blouse, but should it be a skirt or jeans? Maybe the first day she'd dress a bit and wear a skirt. Margery and Florence said they might; and Mary Jane always wore skirts. With cold weather coming, they'd be in pants and heavy clothes soon enough.

When Barbara went downstairs, Jessica was

drinking her coffee and reading a journal. Barbara was reminded of her first morning at school here last year. She had been starting a new school then, too. But how much different things were now.

"Hi, Barb. You look nice," said Jessica smiling. "I'll give you a lift to school for your first day."

That, too, was like last year. "Thanks. Can you wait till I feed the dogs?"

Her mother nodded. "Take your time. I don't have to be at the clinic until eight-thirty. I think I'll have another cinnamon roll."

The rolls smelled yeasty and spicy; Barbara sniffed vigorously as she went into the kitchen. Caliban and Choto waited expectantly on the back porch; they were absolutely certain that she would be bringing out their meal. It must be nice, she thought, to be able to be so trusting. As she poured out the dried pellets, mixed water and extra vitamins with them, she thought back to times when she had wished she were a dog or cat. Life would be so simple then. On the other hand, it was also so dependent. She guessed she preferred the intricacies of being human.

She put down the food bowls, watched Ramon mowing, and savored the morning sunshine before joining her mother for her own breakfast. They didn't dawdle especially, and soon were in the car heading out for the day. Measle watched them go from the porch step.

"Well, here you are starting another school," said Jessica as she backed smoothly out of the drive. Since the disastrous attempt with the car last winter, Barbara had a new appreciation of driving as a skill.

"Un huh. But I'll miss Miss McNealy."

"Yes. She's a good teacher. I'm glad I had a chance to meet her."

"She's great. And, boy, could she keep us in line." Barbara grinned reminiscently. "No tricks there."

Jessica laughed. "I don't know whether you take after your father or me. We'll have to tell you sometime about one or two of our escapades."

It was Barbara's turn to be surprised. "You and Dad got into trouble?"

"Not together. We didn't meet until I was a med student and he was a resident. But we weren't hatched full grown M.D.'s, you know."

"But you both are always so cool and in control —at least most of the time." She remembered the scene in the police station. Once in a while, her mother did, too, get upset."

Jessica shrugged. "Who'd have confidence in a surgeon who became hysterical? It goes with the territory and maybe—sometimes—it rubs off into our personal life."

She stopped to allow an army of teenagers to cross the street. They carried notebooks and looked unusually polished and pressed. Barbara was glad she had decided to dress up a bit.

"I'll get out here, Mom. Then you don't have to get closer in this mob."

"All right." Jessica patted Barbara's knee. "You look fine. You'll do great. Good luck."

"Thanks. And thanks for the ride. See you tonight."

260

Quickly she opened the door and slid out. Her mother drove away, and Barbara joined the group surging toward the large brick building around the corner. She looked for someone she knew, but didn't see anyone. Well, it didn't really matter. She'd know someone at school.

"Hey, Brains! Wait up." It was Ned. He was so slicked-up even his hair was combed in place. "Who do you have for homeroom?"

"Catlett—Room 201. Who do you have?"

"Henderson in 115." He chuckled and grimaced. "Boys on one floor, girls on another."

"That's dumb."

"Sure it is. Don't expect sense out of authorities. But Margery's been checking. She says she thinks our whole group is together for all classes except girls' home ec and boys' wood shop."

"What if I want wood shop?"

He groaned and struck his forehead. "Trust you to try to rock the boat."

They reached the school steps. Ned pointed toward a side door, and she could see the rest of the group clustered there waiting. With Ned beside her, she waved a greeting and ran up the steps to the new year.